Patience
of **Dearing Bay**

Patience
of Dearing Bay

EFFIE FAHEY

CAITLIN PRESS
Prince George, BC
1996

Patience of Dearing Bay
Copyright © 1996 Effie Fahey

Caitlin Press Inc.
P.O. Box 2387, Stn. B
Prince George, B.C. V2N 2S6

All rights reserved. No part of this book may be reproduced in any form by any means without the written permission of the publisher, except by the reviewer, who may quote passages in a review.
Caitlin Press gratefully acknowledges the financial support of the Canada Council and the British Columbia Cultural Services Branch, Ministry of Tourism, Small Business and Culture.

Cover art and illustrations by Gaye Hammond.
All characters appearing in this work are fictional.

Canadian Cataloguing in Publication Data

Fahey, Effie, 1954-
Patience of Dearing Bay

ISBN 0-920576-57-5

I.Title.
PS8561.A54P37 1996   C813'.54   C96-910210-0
PR9199.3.F35P37 1996

*Inspired by my grandparents
Lewis and Emma Coates*

For Christina Fahey and Ronald Fahey

Special thanks to Louise Donnelly

Contents

1. Grandfather Seeks Help *1*
2. Dearing Bay *3*
3. Elizabeth's Labour *5*
4. Best Midwife on the Rock *9*
5. A Queer Looking Face *14*
6. The Bonding *20*
7. Magic Uncle Matthew *23*
8. A Game Called Carpenter *28*
9. A Real Tomboy *31*
10. My Favourite Place *35*
11. A Stranger at Our Door *46*
12. Our Annual Valentine Box *50*
13. My Spotted Friend *56*
14. Kingsley *60*
15. The Price of Carelessness *69*
16. The Secret *74*
17. Andrew's Cove *81*
18. Jake the Snake *87*
19. Learning Goes Beyond the Classroom *91*
20. Troubled Times *100*
21. The Winds of Change *109*
22. High School *114*
23. Matthew's Graduation *122*
24. Off to Toronto *128*
25. The Telegram *135*
26. The Wedding *141*
27. Always in Your Heart *145*

CHAPTER 1

Grandfather Seeks Help

"Tom, 'itch the 'orses quick! Elizabeth needs a midwife right away," Grandmother cried. "Oh Lord, why didn't she say something earlier? Of all da nights to have da baby!"

Grandfather stopped long enough to squeeze his only daughter's clammy hand. How he hated to see her in such pain. "Hold on, me love, daddy will git Aunt Mary."

Grandmother's clinched knuckles turned white beneath her chin. "Godspeed, Tom."

Grandfather forced open the porch door into the howling northern gale force winds blowing off the frozen bay. It was pitch black. He couldn't see his hand in front of him. Sleeting snow felt like needles in his eyes and on his exposed skin. In places the drifts were ten feet high. It wouldn't be easy to get around the cove in this blizzard. Grandfather was glad Grandmother couldn't see his face as he made his way to the barn.

Prince and Queen where reluctant to leave their warm shelter. But the horses could sense Grandfather's urgency and were soon hitched up. Grandfather climbed onto the sleigh dressed in a bear skin jacket that hung to his knees, a fur cap and a thick Newfoundland green and white tartan scarf wrapped around his face. He had a shovel, extra hay and a heavy woollen blanket, just in case. "Gee-up. Gee-up," he shouted, his voice barely heard above the wind. "You must be me eyes and me ears tonight, me friends."

The horses swung their heads high, lunging their strong bodies and long legs forward into the dark. Man and beast, using their brain and brawn, knew they had their work cut out for them. It was impossible to see anything, but Grandfather could tell by the familiar twists and turns in the road they were headed in the right direction. Under normal circumstances a horse ride on the old woodroad was enjoyable, but tonight the three-mile trip to Aunt Mary's house seemed endless.

Along some stretches the wind had blown the freshly-fallen snow off the old woodroad's icy base. Here, the horses galloped at full speed and Grandfather's spirits would soar. Then they'd come to places where the drifted snow rubbed the horses' bellies. Panting and sweating, Prince and Queen were forced to labour their way through while Grandfather gently urged them on. Sometimes he had to clear a passage with the shovel. He refused to think of what would happen if they couldn't make it around the cove. He could not fail. He had made a promise.

He'd bring Aunt Mary to Elizabeth, if it was the last thing he ever did.

CHAPTER 2

Dearing Bay

DEARING BAY, a quiet little outport in Newfoundland, was settled by the Dearings prior to the turn of the eighteenth century. They sailed across the Atlantic from England in their wretched little sailboats, maneuvering through ice flows and along fog-bound coasts. They built their first houses from trees they'd sawed and chopped by hand. Many gave up their lives to the cold Atlantic, the often furious and unforgiving ocean that fed the island inhabitants. Their closest neighbours, native people who couldn't speak their language, were sometimes unfriendly. But the Dearings, proud and blessed with a wonderful sense of humour, were determined to make it at all costs.

In 1952 Dearing Bay was far from modern. There were no doctors or police. Teachers were difficult to come by. Homes were without electricity, indoor plumbing or telephones. There were no automobiles. A single road, wide enough for a couple of horse sleighs to pass, followed the water edge from one end of the village to the other. Horses and sheep ran wild and often grazed upon the tender shoots of green grass that grew in the centre of the road. The two hundred residents of Dearing Bay depended on the river boat, and horse and dog teams for transportation.

Grandmother and Grandfather were born and raised there, not more than two miles apart. They were childhood friends who fell in love and later married in the small white church near the mouth of the Goose River. Rose was twenty-one. Tom was twenty-five. Birds sang on their wedding day, the fields were alive with bumble bees and June flowers, the blue sky was cloudless and only a slight westerly breeze blew off the bay. The whole village turned out to witness their vows – to love, honour and obey until death would part them.

Tonight, the residents of Dearing Bay watched the worst storm of the winter through their windows. Elizabeth Dearing, expecting her baby any day now, was on everyone's mind. As the icy snow glanced off the panes, there was nothing they could do but pray.

Dear God, have mercy. Keep the Dearings safe this night.

CHAPTER 3

Elizabeth's Labour

ELIZABETH HAD CHALKED UP her earlier discomfort to gas. It didn't occur to her she was in labour. Why would it? Pregnancy was private and Elizabeth had never discussed it – not even with her own mother.

She tried to sleep but the infrequent sharp pain nagged just enough to keep her awake. She shifted her weight from side to side; she lay in different positions; she took some medicine for heartburn and told herself to relax. She would think of pleasant experiences – her very first bike ride with her favourite uncle came to mind.

Pain cut through her stomach and lower back and quickly brought her back to reality.

Am I in labour? I can't be – not with the weather like this! Think pleasant thoughts, Elizabeth. Think! Think! Think!

She remembered her sixth birthday. Her father had given her Sarah, the prettiest doll she had ever seen. Sarah wore a gorgeous pink and white frilly dress with delicate lace collar and sleeves that looked too expensive to be touched by the human hand. She had long blond hair, a smiling face and blue eyes that closed when Elizabeth laid her down.

Elizabeth looked over at Sarah who was sitting in an old brown rocking chair in the corner of the bedroom. She seemed to be staring directly into Elizabeth's face. Tonight Sarah's usually happy face looked sad. No matter how hard she tried, Elizabeth could not bring the doll's smile back. In desperation, she hobbled across the room, picked up Sarah without paying any attention to her fine lace collar and sleeves, and turned her face towards the wall.

Another contraction! This one was long, and took its time fading away.

Elizabeth concentrated on her surroundings. She counted every blue and pink flower and green leaf on the bedroom wallpaper. She counted every nail head in the white painted ceiling boards above her bed. She tried to imagine how many coats of paint it would take to hide their imprints forever.

All was in vain. There was no way of escaping her misery. Her insides were being ripped apart.

She prayed to God to deliver her from this living hell. Instead, her torture increased. Somewhere along the way, she must have sinned terribly.

Elizabeth knew she took the Lord's name in vain on occasion. She lied to her mother, swore she didn't smoke any of the cigarettes that went missing from one of the uncle's bedrooms. She also remembered getting angry with her mother a few times and wishing her dead, but now she couldn't recollect why. Then there were all those lies two years ago about going to church Sunday evenings. Instead, she was dating Patrick, a Catholic boy, whom her parents had forbid her to see.

Elizabeth was brought up in the Anglican faith. The people of Dearing Bay frowned upon those that mingled with folk of a different faith. But Elizabeth didn't care. She married Patrick. For awhile it was tough on everyone. Grandfather and the uncles were proud Orangemen who marched to "Onward Christian Soldiers" while Patrick, and his family, visited the Knights of Columbus on a frequent basis. Elizabeth loved Patrick dearly and in the end their love for each other was what counted.

Tears filled her eyes as she remembered Patrick's love and his gentle touch. *Patrick, me love – I can't take dis no longer.* She rolled her knees toward her chest in an attempt to ease her suffering.

Could the old parson, who gave her a good scolding about marrying a Catholic boy, be right when he said it was a sin in the eyes of God? Was she getting her just reward?

What nonsense is going through me head. Elizabeth flung aside the old parson's silly words.

A razor-sharp pain pierced her lower abdomen, squeezing slowly through her stomach and lower back, taking her breath away. Her knees knocked together, uncontrollable. Perspiration trickled down from her hairline. She was scared to inhale deeply. Another contraction and another. They were coming closer together. She was convinced God had turned his back on her. Unable to stand her misery alone any longer, she turned to someone who she knew would be there for her – even if God wasn't.

"Mother, I think I's dying!"

That's when Grandmother jumped out of her warm bed. A glance at Elizabeth, frothing through the mouth like a bull moose in rutting season, had sent cold shivers up and down her spine.

Five hours later, Grandmother looked yet another time at the clock slowing ticking above her head. The long hand had moved one minute. *Where is you two, Tom?*

For a split second the thought of Tom and the horses in an accident entered her mind, but she thrust it away as quickly as it came. She had to deal with the harsh reality that Elizabeth just might not hang on much longer. She prayed and prayed while longing to hear Tom's footsteps and Aunt Mary's familiar voice. She knew too well that if they didn't arrive soon it would be too late for Elizabeth.

Elizabeth entered her final stages of labour. Her body was screaming at her to push with all of her might. She pushed and pushed and pushed and yet her baby refused to budge from her warm womb. Elizabeth's strength was ebbing along with the early morning tides that drained the shoreline of its water. Part of her wanted to let go and embrace the darkness with open arms, but a determined inner voice told her to hang on, to fight.

Grandmother wiped Elizabeth's sweaty face with a cold cloth. "Don't give up, me child. Aunt Mary will be here soon. She will have yur baby born in no time at all."

Elizabeth paid no heed. She could feel the darkness descend upon her.

CHAPTER 4

Best Midwife on the Rock

GRANDFATHER REACHED AUNT MARY'S house just before dawn. A few more hours and the sun would be coming up.

Aunt Mary's kerosene lamp flickered from the storm when she opened her door. Grandfather's face told her everything. "Elizabeth?"

He nodded his head. "Yes tis."

"Step inside and get warm while I git me things."

He rubbed his hands together over the stove. The heat felt good.

Sixty-five-year-old Aunt Mary was the finest in her field. The best midwife on the rock is what the locals called her. She had been bringing babies into the world for over thirty years. And a new baby always made her heart sing. The closest doctor was at least forty miles away and accessible only by dog team during the winter months. He was a doctor by name but people had their doubts that he rated as highly as Aunt Mary when it came to borning a child. The common saying was that men depended upon Aunt Mary a great deal more than women at times like these. Childbirth, a woman's thing, left men feeling inadequate. They took comfort in knowing Aunt Mary was in charge.

There had been unhappy endings too. Thank goodness they were few and far between. The deafening silence of death – a stillborn baby, a dead mother or both – God forbid, was heart breaking for everyone.

Grandfather and Aunt Mary had gone about a mile when the storm let up. Daylight was just about to break. It was easier to see where they were going now, but Aunt Mary's experience told her babies liked to venture into the world with the rising sun. This made her uneasy. *Dear God, don't let Elizabeth's baby be too impatient.*

"Whoa!" Prince and Queen stopped dead in their tracks.

"What's da matter, Tom?"

"Da road is blocked. Looks like da old spruce tree is falled over from da wind."

"Lord 'elp us."

Grandfather shovelled snow while Aunt Mary dug swiftly with her hands and arms. They moved the tree just enough to give them room to pass. They both could have done with a rest after, but that would have to come later. Aunt Mary glanced towards the sun when she climbed back on the sleigh. It was nearly full in the eastern sky.

Prince and Queen were slowing down. Grandfather continued to urge them on. Scattered lazy snowflakes stuck to his frozen mittens holding their reins. They melted when they landed on the exhausted horses. It couldn't be much farther, could it? At last, the pale yellow house came in view. Grey smoke rose heavenward toward the morning sun. It was a welcoming sight. But what would they find inside?

Best Midwife on the Rock

Grandmother was at the sleigh before the horses stopped. "Looks like she's almost gived up fer death."

Grandfather dropped his cold face into his icy mittens.

"I'll hear none of dat nonsense," said Aunt Mary. She grabbed her bag and followed Grandmother inside.

She squeezed Elizabeth's hand. "It's Aunt Mary," she said. "It's going to be ar'right."

Grandmother washed Elizabeth's face with ice cold water fresh from the water barrel. Elizabeth moaned, her eyes rolling to the back of her head.

"Elizabeth, you got to help me now." Aunt Mary gently bent Elizabeth's knees until her feet were flat on the bed. "Yur daddy – he's been in da blizzard 'most da night and dis morning. He wants to see hes grandchild soon." She placed two large pillows behind Elizabeth's back. "Yur baby got a mind of her own – I'd say, me darling. Jest like her poor father, eh."

Grandmother continued to wipe the sweat off Elizabeth's brow. "Pay heed to Aunt Mary."

"I's going to use me hands a bit now child. Pay no attention to what I dos." Aunt Mary moved to the foot of the bed. "Don't use up yur strength now, child. Aunt Mary will tell you when to push."

Aunt Mary could see the baby's blond head. She forced her long bony fingers inside Elizabeth's battered and bruised body. She grabbed, pulled and twisted the unborn child. Elizabeth was barely conscious yet her wretched body screamed for her to push. Aunt Mary sternly instructed her otherwise.

Finally! Aunt Mary gave the signal. "Push, push, push."

Elizabeth mustered all of her remaining strength.

The sounds of a crying baby filled the room – a crying baby girl.

"God love us," said Grandmother.

After Aunt Mary tended to the baby and Grandmother tended to Elizabeth, Aunt Mary said, "I could do with a good cup'a tea Rose, me dear."

"First," said Grandmother, "how about a good strong drink of Tom's rum."

CHAPTER 5

A Queer Looking Face

THE BABY THAT SENT GRANDFATHER out into a mid-January blizzard was me. Naturally, I don't remember anything about my birth, the circumstances leading up to it, or, for that matter, any of my very early childhood. However, once I was old enough to understand, my grandparents, Tom and Rose Dearing, told me everything.

That January morning Grandfather, not knowing I had been born a few minutes before, looked at his pocket watch one more time. It was seven sharp. Only an hour had passed since he and Aunt Mary had arrived. It felt like a lifetime ago, yet he had kept himself busy. He watered, fed and brushed the horses. He shovelled the previous day's manure outside. He even mended some harnesses that had needed repairs for quite some time.

What use is a man in times like this?

If Grandfather were to let his emotions rule his male judgment, he would be in his daughter's room, holding her hand and comforting her just like he did when she was a little girl.

Instead he was alone with his memories. *My dear Elizabeth, I wish we could do it all over again. I would take more time to appreciate things. Like the birthday cake you baked for my fortieth birthday, our walks along the beach, watching the sun set in front of the log cabin after a long day fishing, your excitement at Christmas. And Patrick. Why did I try to keep you apart over religion?*

"Tom! Tom!"

Grandmother poked her head around the barn door. "Elizabeth's going to be ar'right. She has a healthy baby girl."

"She do?" Grandfather swallowed hard. "Well, da Lord bless us." He tried to wipe his eyes without Grandmother noticing.

Grandmother turned and looked outside. "When you's ready come on in and see yur granddaughter." She knew her husband handled his emotions best in private and closed the door behind her.

Grandfather could feel the hot tears building up in his eyes. *Was it his grandfather or his father or was it both who told him only weak men cried?* Weak or not, he could not hold back any longer. Like broken dams, tears of joy streamed down his cheeks, trickling into the corners of his mouth.

Finally all cried out, he strolled over to Prince and Queen who were resting in their stalls. Their sweaty bodies had cooled down. They were no longer panting. "Did you hear what Rose said? A baby girl. And, Elizabeth is ar'right." He rubbed their white-patched faces and muscular necks. "I don't know what I'd done without you, me friends. I jest don't know." They nuzzled his hand as if they understood. "I have me first grandchild – a girl. Elizabeth did ar'right, eh."

Queen neighed in agreement.

Grandfather felt like a brand-new man. He stepped outside and took a deep breath of the crisp morning air. The storm had passed. The bright yellow sun was shining in the clear, blue sky. Grandmother's tracks to and from the house were the only visible marks on the blanket of fresh white snow. The snow-laden spruce trees along the pathway from the barn looked like Christmas cookies covered with white icing. Thick white caps curled around the roof of the house. Grey and white smoke towered from the chimney into the early morning sky.

His eyes, as blue as the sky above him, took in the surrounding wintry beauty. Mother Nature was one unpredictable lady, wasn't she? Only she could create a masterpiece out of a terrible storm; only she could be a man's worst enemy as well as his good friend; only she could create or take a life as quickly as a fairy could wave a magic wand. Certainly her powers were not to be judged by mere mortals.

He opened the door to the smell of frying bacon and eggs, mingled with the aroma of toasted homemade bread. His mouth watered. He hadn't had as much as a cup of tea or a slice of bread since an early supper the night before. But breakfast would have to wait. He had more important matters to attend to. He must introduce himself to me, his grandchild.

Grandfather removed his winter clothes and boots, walked into his bedroom, washed up and changed into a clean white cotton shirt, narrow black tie and black woollen slacks. He shaved off his day-old stubble and combed what remained of a thick crop of hair. He looked at himself in the old square mirror hanging above the wash basin.

"Dis will do." One more quick check in the mirror. "Yeah, dis will do."

Elizabeth's door was left open to allow the heat from the old Franklin wood stove to take the chill out of the air. Grandfather quietly entered her bedroom. Elizabeth was sleeping like a newborn baby herself. Her dark brown hair curled loosely around her oval face. Her normally rosy cheeks and glowing skin were ashen. How his beloved daughter had suffered. Grandfather sat gently beside her and held her work-hardened hand in his. He caressed her forehead. Elizabeth opened her eyes for a moment. "Daddy." Then she drifted off to sleep again.

Grandfather bent down and kissed her pale cheek. "God only knows what you's been through." He tucked the hand sewn quilt around her shoulders, then tiptoed towards the little white cradle just outside her door where I was sleeping.

That was the same cradle that my mother and all of his other children had used before me. About a month before, Mother had dug it out of the old storage shed. She cleaned and painted it until it looked brand new. Out of some leftover materials Grandmother had around she made a mattress and matching blankets trimmed with ribbons in pink and blue so they could go equally well for a girl or a boy.

As Grandfather had watched Mother work on the cradle, old memories flooded back. The cradle was handmade by his father-in-law, who was the best finish carpenter in the community. Grandfather remembered how surprised Rose was the night her father handed it to her. How could he know? She had told no one that she was expecting. She was only in her third month and too early to show. Even to this day, Grandfather had never told her that it was he who had whispered the wonderful news in her father's ear.

He remembered when Alan, his first, was born and how little and helpless he seemed. How Alan loved to sleep in the little white cradle.

His second son, Ivan, never liked the cradle but preferred to sleep with him and Rose.

Daniel, the third child, died in his sleep at the age of three months.

Less than a year after Daniel's passing, the little cradle was filled with love and laughter again. He had been blessed with a daughter. How he had longed for a little girl!

Just after Elizabeth's sixteenth birthday, the cradle was in use again for their youngest son, Matthew. He was truly a surprise. My grandparents were getting on in years and never expected to have another child. They were so thankful for little Matthew who helped them stay young at heart.

Grandfather bent over the little cradle – the little cradle with all its joy and pain – and saw me for the very first time. "Oh me darling. What a sweet thing you is! A face like yur mother's and all dat yellow hair like yur fa–" He didn't finish his sentence but looked towards Mother's door, hoping he hadn't been overheard.

Others may have said that I looked like a skinned rabbit but Grandfather saw only smooth skin, dainty features and perfect hands and fingernails. "Oh my –

you don't look like a newborn at all – nar wrinkle, nar bit a puffiness and yur face ain't one bit red." He touched my cheek with his finger. "You is a Dearing ar'right – just like yur mother before you."

Knowing I was being admired for my inherited beauty, I chose to show off a bit. I crinkled my wee nose. I yawned. I sucked my perfect hands with my little pink mouth. I whimpered like a puppy. Finally, I used my lungs to their full potential.

"Shhhhh, Pap is here." Grandfather bent his tall, straight body over the little white cradle and picked me up with his strong arms. His gentle blue eyes proudly watched my face while I cried. He rocked me back and forth, one hand holding my blond head. *"Oh sweet baby, please don't cry, Pappy will bring you a rocking toy."* I settled down and stopped bawling. I tried, without success, to focus my large eyes on his face. They crossed like two rising moons.

Smiling, he held me close to his chest. "Well now, dat's some queer looking face."

CHAPTER 6

The Bonding

MY MOTHER CALLED ME PATIENCE. Many of my friends were called after some family relative, but the name Patience was unheard of in my village until I was given the handle. I have speculated about Mother's reason. The truth is, I will never know why she chose it because all I know about my mother is what my grandparents have told me. Except for one very descriptive story that took place a few days after my birth told to me by Aunt Mary.

Aunt Mary had ended up stranded at the Dearings. Another snowstorm had hit and it would take days before people were mobile again. Grandmother didn't mind at all. She could do with the company and she certainly could do with the help. Mother was too weak to look after me or, for that matter, herself. And four-year-old Matthew was a handful at the best of times.

Aunt Mary took over getting Mother back on her feet. She allowed her to sleep for the best part of two days, making sure Mother drank plenty of fluids and ate the food that she brought. She insisted that Mother take cod liver oil pills and blood tonic four times a day.

On day three, Aunt Mary greeted Mother with a mission in mind. "A bit a colour in your face, eh," she said, pinching Mother's cheeks.

The Bonding

"Oh, Aunt Mary, I's feeling a lot better," Mother said, sitting up without help.

"Dat's good." Aunt Mary handed her a breakfast tray. Her eyes were on Mother's nightgown, soiled with breast milk.

"I could eat a horse right now," said Mother, filling her mouth with home-made beans.

"You best eat fast cause da baby is starting to fuss," said Aunt Mary. "When is dat child going to get a name, Elizabeth? I's sick of calling her da baby."

"Soon," said Mother. "Can't make up me mind what to call her."

Aunt Mary carried out the breakfast tray, and returned with me, kicking and screaming in her arms. "She's hungry, poor little thing," she said, handing me to Mother. "Stick your teat in her mouth and she'll shut up."

Mother's eyes grew as wide as saucers. She stared at Aunt Mary as if she had two heads. "What?"

"You heard me, Elizabeth," said Aunt Mary. "No point in all dat good milk going to waste."

"Breast feeding is not for me," said Mother. "Get me a bottle."

Aunt Mary closed the door to Mother's bedroom. "Elizabeth, you must bond with yur child." She waved her finger back and forth close to Mother's face. "Now do as I tell you."

Mother had never given any thought to breast feeding. That was for animals in the barnyard. What was wrong with a bottle? I had done quite fine over the last few days without human milk. A picture of a young lamb grabbing and hauling on its mother's teat came to her mind. She cringed. She looked over at Aunt Mary, who sat facing her, arms folded tightly around her chest. Slowly, knowing Aunt Mary wasn't going to give up, Mother unbuttoned her nightgown and turned my face awkwardly to her bosom.

"Much better," said Aunt Mary.

Instinctively, my little pink face nuzzled Mother's naked breast. I wrapped my hungry mouth around her nipple. Mother's body was as stiff as a board. It would not give me the nourishment I wanted. I turned my head away, crying with hunger pains.

"Relax, Elizabeth. Tis a natural thing to do."

"She doesn't like it," said Mother, sitting perfectly straight. "I's trying to relax. Just give me a bottle, will you?"

"Sometimes it takes time," said Aunt Mary. "Just have a little bit of patience."

Aunt Mary worked with Mother, coaching her all the way. Little by little Mother and I worked things out. She stroked my blond hair, my forehead and my face while I sucked, and then slept. The barnyard images were replaced by a wonderful feeling of maternal love.

"Dat's much better," Aunt Mary said. "Look how happy da little one is – as contented as a bird in its nest."

Suddenly, my knees came up to my chest, my eyes turned red and filled with water. I moaned and groaned.

"Oh, my God," said Mother, holding her nose.

"Dat's your beans working on her," said Aunt Mary, walking towards Mother, arms held out. "I'll take da baby and change her."

"I'll do it, Aunt Mary," said Mother. She kissed my cheek. "If dat's all right with you, little Patience."

CHAPTER 7

Magic Uncle Matthew

PRIOR TO MY ARRIVAL, Matthew had spent many hours with Mother. He especially liked to help her at the general store where she worked.

"Matthew, would you be me big helper at da store today?"

He would jump up and down with joy while Mother dragged the boxes over to him. "Put da tins of soup on da bottom shelves fer me, Matthew."

He would sit on the worn wooden floor between the shelves, and stack for hours. He placed each can in a row making sure the red and white labels were facing out, like Mother had shown him. "I dare say, I'll be starving fer a jawbreaker by the time I's done, Sis." Jawbreakers were Matthew's favourite. They came in so many colours and lasted for a long time.

She would smile and ruffle his hair. "As soon as you's finished, you can pick out da biggest jawbreaker in da store."

In the summer, Mother would take Matthew on bike rides, up and down the village path. She played his favourite game, hide-and-seek, and baked him treats nearly every Saturday. She played ball with him. She ran and jumped and wrestled him to the ground. She listened to his stories and often tucked him in at nights.

Strangers often thought Matthew was her son, not her brother.

On the morning of my birth, Matthew heard noises coming from Mother's room that sounded like two fighting tom cats. The wailing sounds I was making intrigued him. He raced from his bedroom down the hallway to find out what was going on. He met Aunt Mary in Mother's doorway. She was holding a small bundle – a bundle that wiggled and squawked. His first thought was that Aunt Mary had caught the tom cats. And that she was going to do away with them for making such awful noise.

Matthew's mouth fell open. "What's dat you have, Aunt Mary?"

"A baby, Matthew. A wee baby girl," she said, bending down to show him what she had inside the bundle. "Would you like to see her?"

"A baby? A baby girl?" His eyes grew wide. "Where did you get her?"

"Dis's Elizabeth's baby. She was jest born," said Aunt Mary, pulling the blanket away from my face. "Matthew, she's made you an uncle. You's Uncle Matthew now."

"Where did Sis get her?" he said, coming closer to make sure I was for real. "Where did Sis get her?" His eyes narrowed, looking up at Aunt Mary.

"Got her from da rotten stump, of course." All young children were told babies were found in old tree stumps. Aunt Mary walked toward the kitchen table, leaving Matthew with his many questions standing alone, by Mother's door.

He raced into her room. "Wake up, Sis," he said, pushing on her shoulder. "Sis, wake up."

Mother stirred in her exhaustion but didn't answer him.

He left, closing the door behind him. He had never seen his sister so tired before. *Uncle Matthew.* He practised saying it over and over. He liked how the words rolled off his tongue. He climbed up on a kitchen chair to get a better look at me. Aunt Mary let him touch my face and hands gently while she bathed me with lukewarm water. "What's wrong with her belly button?"

"Oh, all babies got dat. It'll git better."

"She has no pee-pee like mine."

Aunt Mary's eyes twinkled. "Dat's because she's a girl. Boys and girls have different pee-pees, Matthew."

"Why?"

"God made dem dat way. No more questions now, hear."

"Yes, Aunt Mary."

For the next few days, Matthew stayed fairly close to my cradle or close to whoever was holding me. My grandparents explained as best as they could. But he had things to ask his sister. She always told him the truth.

As soon as Mother was well enough, she invited Matthew for the talk he longed for. She ran her fingers through his hair. "How's da best boy in da world?"

"Okay," Matthew said, looking down, picking at his fingers.

"Got something on yur mind?" said Mother, lifting his chin with her thumb. "Want to tell Sis about it?"

"Da baby."

"Da baby.... Patience?"

"All she does is pee and pooh," he said. "And cry." Matthew's bottom lip went out. "Mom and Dad takes her up, all the time. You going to keep her, Sis?"

"Yes Matthew, I's keeping her," said Mother, her eyes never leaving his face. "But, you is still me favourite boy." She sat Matthew on her lap.

"Aunt Mary says you got her in the old rotten stump," said Matthew. "That true?"

Mother hesitated.

At fourteen she had still believed babies were found in old tree stumps. She was shocked when she learned where they actually came from. To add to her embarrassment, only a few months before she had spent hours digging out an old stump. She had even told her teacher that there must have been something wrong with that particular stump, because there wasn't a trace of anything to resemble a baby.

For now, Mother when along with Aunt Mary's fib. She vowed one day when Matthew was older, she would explain everything to him. She would tell him about sex, pregnancy and birth – the real facts of life!

"Why did you look fer a baby?" said Matthew. I guess, since Mother had said nothing, he assumed she found me in a rotten stump.

"Eh ... I guess God wanted me to find her."

"God?" said Matthew, his nose rumpling up.

"Maybe he felt dat a little girl would be fun to have around," said Mother. "Fer you to play with, Matthew."

"She's too small to play with," he said, but his eyes sparkled a little.

"How about if you held her," said Mother, setting me on his lap. She showed him how to support my head and back, explaining how I had to be handled carefully, so I wouldn't get hurt. "She'll grow up soon, Matthew. And she'll be lots of fun."

Matthew's face came alive. "She's some wiggly, Sis," he said, beaming from ear to ear.

"Patience makes you a very special boy," said Mother. "You's now Uncle Matthew and dat sure sounds grown-up to me."

Matthew gave her his widest smile.

"She likes you, Matthew," said Mother, smiling back at him. "I've never seen her so quiet. You must have magic in you, lad."

"Really Sis?" he said, looking at me, and giggling. "Uncle Matthew is magic, little Patience."

CHAPTER 8

A Game Called Carpenter

MATTHEW ACTED MORE like an older brother than an uncle. When I was really little, I used to do mostly what he wanted. As I grew older, I got better at getting my own way but I had to be on my toes at all times.

"My turn to play Pap," I said. Matthew and I were playing Carpenter, a game we had invented. I was hoping that he wouldn't remember that I played Pap last time. Whoever played Pap got to use lots of words that we couldn't dare say in earshot of an adult, or anyone who would blab.

Matthew folded his arms and leaned against the camp he had built from leftover pieces of lumber and board. "It's my turn," he said. "Besides, boys should play that part – not girls."

"Not girls," I mimicked. "Girls can do anything boys can do."

"No, they can't," said Matthew.

"They can," I said. "And girls are smarter too."

"Boys should do boy things," said Matthew. "And girls should do girl things."

"I'm playing Pap next time or I won't play at all," I said.

"All right, Patience," said Matthew.

I jumped right into my part. "Tom, I've been thinking, we should do a little renovation. We need to move that door six feet two inches from where it is – towards the window. And move that wall back three feet four inches. Leaves enough space to build a little sewing room for me."

"Damn it Rose," Matthew said, "only last year you had me move the door. And move the wall where it is now. Is there no end in sight? I have been shifting stuff around this place every since we been married. Good Lord, woman, you'll drive me in the ground yet."

With my left hand, I removed my pretend eyeglasses. "Tom, this will be the last time. I know exactly what I want. I see it clearly in my head. I tell you, Tom," I said, pretending to put my glasses back on. "There won't be much to it – a few days work at the most."

"Okay Rose, I'll get started right away." Matthew looked down at the floor and shook his head just like Pap did when he knew there was no way out for him. With tools in hand, Matthew squinted with one eye and estimated where the door should be relocated. He pretended to cut a hole in the wall.

"Good God, Tom! You didn't even measure it." I began pacing back and forth. "That wall is too far back. The board is too long. Look at the door hole. It's too far to the left." I spoke louder and faster and waved my hands in the air.

Matthew's hammer picked up speed. He nailed harder and harder. Indentations patterned the wall just like Pap's did when Nan voiced her desire for perfection. Matthew pretended the hammer missed and landed on his finger. He danced around the camp. He shook his hand back and forth. A string of curse words poured from his mouth. Normally, Matthew and I would not dare say such words but it didn't seem so sinful when we repeated what Pap said.

"I could do a better job myself." I scurried around the room. I touched every nail head and dent Matthew had made in the wood. "A lot better job myself."

Matthew still cursing, we continued our exaggerated comedy of my grandparents.

"Your language is wicked. That's why nobody comes to help out – people are afraid of you." I drew my eyebrows together and pulled my face tight.

Matthew threw his hammer across the camp. "Son of a codfish's arse."

CHAPTER 9

A Real Tomboy

"Pap, may Matthew and I help?" Pap was stacking wood in the woodhouse.

"Sure, me darling," Pap said. "Could do with da help."

Matthew and I took turns picking out pieces of wood. We lugged over a huge sticky piece of fir and dropped it next to Pap's feet. I raced ahead and found another piece. "I've got one."

"You picked out the last three pieces, Patience, now it's my turn," said Matthew.

"So what," I said, lifting it up on its side. "Come on, help me out, will you. It's too heavy for me."

"Just this one time, Patience, then it's my turn." Matthew seemed to be a wee bit annoyed.

"You snooze, you lose, Matthew," I said, eyeing another piece. "You are such a slow poke today."

"I'm not," said Matthew. "You're showing off."

"Patience! Matthew! No more dat or git outside and play," said Pap. We knew he was serious so I let Matthew have his turn.

I watched Pap work with each piece of wood. "Why do you pile it so carefully?"

"You dos it dis way 'cause if a whole tier floundered, could hurt you." *Clunk*. He fitted another piece in place. "Dis way, it will never fall."

"Will you show us how you do it, Daddy?" Matthew handed him a piece of wood.

"Dat's too little, son. Give me dat big one."

Matthew and I dragged over the piece he pointed to. Pap dropped it in place and another satisfying clunk echoed throughout the woodhouse.

"Now, hand me the little piece," he said.

I watched him fit it perfectly in place. "Matthew, I got it now. Stacking wood is just like fitting my jumbo jigsaw puzzle together on Nan's kitchen table."

"Can we try now, Daddy?" Matthew seemed to have the idea too.

"I could do with a break. You and Patience go ahead. I'll have a smoke," he said. Pap looked outside at the rain. It had been drizzling off and on all day. The woodhouse was toasty warm already, but Pap put another piece of wood in the tin stove. He hummed an Irish song, tapping his feet now and then. Matthew and I hummed along with him while we hauled and stacked.

Suddenly the door opened and David walked in, cap soaking wet and axe in his hand. "Look what I got for my birthday." David Edwards lived next door with his grandparents. We had been friends for as long as I could remember.

Matthew and I stopped stacking wood to admire the sharp blade and the shiny red finish of the handle. David held it out to Matthew. "It cuts good," he said. "Try it."

Matthew easily split a piece of dry spruce. Then David placed a piece of wood on the chopping block and hit it dead centre. He was almost as good as Matthew. How did David, who was a year younger than me, know how to split wood?

I stomped over to Pap. "Show me how to use the axe." I didn't like it that both boys could do something that I couldn't.

"I can show you, Patience," Matthew and David said in unison.

Pap hid a smile. "Matthew," he said, "git Patience da tomahawk and her own chopping block will you, lad."

Matthew eagerly did as he was told while David dug through the wood pile for a flat dry piece of fir that would be easy to split. "Hold the axe like this, Patience," said Matthew. I watched his left hand slide up the handle to met his right hand. "Then swing like this."

The axe sliced cleanly through the wood and the two gleaming halves fell to the ground. David set one on the chopping block for me.

"That doesn't look too hard," I said, and snatched up the little tomahawk and swung it just like Matthew.

I missed completely.

"Aim before you swing," said David.

I swung again. A splinter flew in the air and the axe stuck in the chopping block. I yanked on the handle with both hands – it would not budge. I pushed over the chopping block and stood with all of my weight on the handle until the blade came free.

Matthew smirked. "Easy, is it? I felt like throwing the tomahawk at him.

Pap positioned my hands and placed his on top of mine. We swung together. The wood split in half, a piece falling on either side of the chopping block. "Let's try it a few more times," he said. I got better with every try. Soon I was doing it all on my own.

Nan opened the door and her smile quickly turned to a frown. "Patience, what are you doing with dat axe?" She scowled at Pap. "Good Lord Tom, don't you have no sense. Da child could cut herself." She took the tomahawk away from me and stuck it safely in the chopping block. "Look at yur hands. Dey is full of blisters and sap. And, look at yur clothes – not fit to be put on yur back again."

Nan motioned me to go ahead of her in the pouring rain. "Go on inside and clean yur hands. Butter should get dat sap off." Nan's eyes narrowed. "I jest don't know what I's going to do with you," she said. "Goodness me, Patience, you is a real tomboy."

Matthew grinned. I gave him the evil eye and marched ahead of Nan.

"Patience," called David, running past Nan to catch me. "Grandpa Edward's woodhouse tomorrow." He looked over his shoulder, making sure Nan wasn't in earshot. "We'll cleave wood all day, eh tomboy."

CHAPTER 10

My Favourite Place

I woke up to Pap tapping me on the shoulder. "Patience. Time to git up and have some breakfast if you is going across da bay with Matthew and me." I was out of bed in a flash. My first trip this salmon season. I could hardly wait to see our rustic log cabin again with its gable roof and rusty tin chimney.

Matthew poked his head around the door. "Yeah, sleepy head, hurry up. The boat is loaded and we are waiting on you." I picked up my clock. It said six. Why didn't the darn alarm go off at five-thirty like it was supposed to?

"Don't wolf yur porridge like dat – you'll be sick," said Nan.

I gobbled the last spoonful. "I'm already late." I grabbed my bag and hurried towards the door.

"Excuse me," said Nan. "Don't I git a hug and a kiss before you leave?"

I wrapped my arms, bag still in hand, around her neck and hugged her tightly. "Why don't you come, Nan?"

"Got too much to do – another time, perhaps."

"But you're going to be all alone all week," I said. I dropped my bag to the floor. My eyes followed. "I could stay if you really want me to." My words came out really slow.

"No, no, dear, you go on and enjoy yurself." Nan picked up my bag and handed it back to me. "It seems to me you'd have more fun across the bay den here cleaning and baking." Nan knew how much I loved being with Pap and Matthew. She also knew how much I hated doing housework.

"Thank you, Nan. I love you." I was off and running.

The white river boat cut through blue-green water smooth as glass. I squealed with delight when we came around the sandbar heading into the cove towards our cabin. Pap cut the motor. The boat slowed. Matthew grabbed a pole and pushed us ashore over familiar rocks and sand.

I jumped out and took a deep breath of fresh air. "This has to be the prettiest place in the whole wide world."

"How would you know, Patience? Not like you have been anywhere besides Dearing Bay," said Matthew. Lately, Matthew was going through a factual phase. It really bugged me at times.

I walked up the path to our one-room cabin. It stood between tall birch trees on a grassy meadow surrounding by yellow, red and blue wildflowers in full bloom. A flock of yellowhammers took flight when I passed in front of them. I stopped at the cherry tree to see if the sparrow's nest was still there. It was. My old friends, the blue jays, sang when I arrived. I checked the berry patch at the edge of the meadow. It would be another good season for strawberries and red currants.

At little later, sitting on the bench in front of the cabin I looked towards the grey-black protruding cliffs that ran out into bay. They were alive with seagulls and ravens. The little island to the north, just beyond the cliffs, was clearly visible. The larger island to the south, where Pap had his salmon nets, loomed at me through the fog. I climbed down the cliffs to the rocky beach below. The water pools were swarming with minnows and sea urchins. A salmon leaped out of the water not more than six feet from the grey shoreline. How lucky I was to live where the ocean provided us food – salmon, sea trout, cod, flounder, lobster, crab and various other species that were too many to name. I picked up a flat rock and skipped it on the bay.

"Tis perfect, Patience. Dat's why I built me cabin here," said Pap, startling me. "Let's go see what it's like on da inside."

Pap opened the little five-foot by two-foot door. He had to duck his head and squeeze through. Matthew and I followed. I threw my bag on one of the rough built-in beds. Matthew threw his bag on the other. Pap swiped his hand across the dusty shelf in the corner where we would store our canned foods and few utensils. Matthew lifted the table which folded against the wall. I positioned its single leg in place to hold it. Pap got the rusty oil lamp off the wall and shook it. It was full of fuel. I took down last year's church calendar hanging over the table and replaced it with a new one. Pap brushed the cobwebs from the ceiling and corners. Matthew swept the floor and threw the dirt in the rusty tin stove sitting on its bed of grey and black rocks.

Later when everything was packed away, I squeezed by the stove to look out the window. There was only one window in the cabin and it was very small.

"I want to look now, Patience," Matthew said.

I choose to ignore him because of his earlier sarcasm. He tried to push me aside but I held my ground. He pushed again and I pushed back. We both lost our balance and fell on top of the old stove. Clattering and clanking, the stove crumpled under our weight. I looked up just in time to see the chimney come apart at the join. "Oh no!" I yelled, soot funnelling towards us.

Pap's agitated blue eyes looked down into our blackened faces. "Now look what you've done." He pushed the chimney back into place. "I should knowed better den to bring da two of you here."

Matthew brushed his clothes. A cloud of soot flew through the air.

"Matthew, git outside and do dat," said Pap, reaching for the broom and dustpan. "Don't you have nar bit of sense left in yur head." Matthew and I dashed for the door at the same time. We tripped over each other, four black-smudged legs and arms waving in the air as we struggled to get outside. "I's not taking da two of you with me, no more. Nar one of you can behave."

I stuck my smeared face back inside. "I'm sorry, Pap," I said, wiping the soot from my eyes. Pap had fixed the stove. He stopped sweeping long enough to acknowledge me with a nod. Was that a smile I saw before he turned his back to me? "It was all my fault, Pap. I promise I'll be good for the rest of the trip."

"I promise I'll be good too," said Matthew, standing behind me.

My Favourite Place

Pap dumped the dustpan. "Tis clean again," he said, slapping his hand on his thigh. "Oh my, dis won't do. Must check me nets. Coming?"

"Not me. I'm going trouting off the rocks," said Matthew.

"I'll go with you," I said.

Pap was a powerful oarsman and I loved to watch him row. Pap had each foot planted on opposite sides of the boat for perfect balance. Bending forward he lifted his oars about fifty-five degrees in the air. Then he dropped both oars in unison into the water. Leaning backwards he used his long arms as extensions for the paddles and the boat steadily picked up speed. I watched the counter-clockwise whirlpools made by the oars. Each disappeared as the blue-and-white wake from the boat widened, erasing the whirlpools. What a pity the artist never got credit for these pretty water sculptures.

We reached the nets far too quickly. The boat ride was my favourite part. While Pap picked kelp from his nets, I watched the ocean's bottom. The fish swimming to and fro were entertaining. I found I could see farther into the deep by looking through the circles made by clasping my forefingers and thumbs.

I imagined I was a friend to all of God's underwater creatures. My fantasy began with me swimming far into the depths of the ocean. I was surrounded with cod, trout, salmon, herring, lobster, squid, crab and flounder. We played fish games such as tag and hide-and-seek. I was the biggest fish in the ocean and I was their leader. I took them close to the shoreline for a lesson that I felt they should learn – a lesson in survival.

I told them all about fishing nets, where they could find them and how to escape from them. I held out a net in front of them. "Picture this wrapped securely around your gills." I went on to explain that they should never try to swim though the net but change directions and swim away. The fish were grateful for my teachings. They invited me back again the next day.

"Patience, Patience, is you sleeping?" My eyes jolted open to see Pap crouched down next to me. "I've been calling yur name o'er and o'er."

"Must had drifted off," I said. There were only two salmon in the boat and I remembered my daydream. Had I jinxed Pap? "Not many salmon running yet, eh?"

"A good southerly wind will bring dem dis direction," said Pap. I was grateful for his response.

Back on land, Pap cleaned his salmon and put them on kelp in the shade of the cabin. Matthew came by showing off his catch, six good-size sea trout. "Let's take a stroll along the beach before we eat," he said. The tide had gone out and kelp crackled under our feet. Squishy sand clung to our boots. Matthew and I picked up a rubber ball, a few colourful bottles and odds and ends that we would add to our cache. Pap found a piece of rope and cork that he could use for his fishing nets. We spotted a moose drinking in one of the many streams. A fox darted in front of us with the remains of a fish in its mouth. We watched trout swimming in a bubbling brook.

"I wish Nan was here," I said.

"She'll come next time," said Pap. "Let's go back, I'm getting a bit hungry."

"I'm in the mood for sea trout," said Matthew. My mouth watered.

My Favourite Place

"I'll race you back, Matthew," I said. He tripped on a wet log, catching his pants and ripping them. I picked up speed and was sitting on the bunk flashing my biggest smile when he crouched through the tiny door.

Pap fried the fish in pork fat and served it with Nan's home-made bread. It tasted almost as good as Christmas dinner. I ate until I hurt.

"Patience, I'll teach you how to row if you will clean the dishes," Matthew said. He hated doing dishes as much as I did.

"Okay."

Matthew could row nearly as well as Pap. I could learn easily from him. Just the other day, I saw Mr. Edwards teaching David how to row. How surprised David would be when he found out that I rowed as well as he could.

The waters were fairly calm and Matthew paddled around the cove to the north. "Watch what I do, Patience. Once we're away from the rocks, you can try."

I sat on the thwart and took the old wooden oars in my hands. They were heavy and clumsy. I positioned myself in the boat the way Pap and Matthew did. Matthew stood behind me and guided my hands and arms until I got the oars moving in unison. "Up. Down. Up. Down. Up. Down."

"Let me try it on my own now." The up-down words continued inside my head. It was awkward at first but it didn't take long for the movement to become natural. "I'm moving straight now," I said. I couldn't keep from giggling.

"Just use one oar and hold the other one under water," said Matthew. "See how you turn."

Before long I was able to steer the boat in any direction and Matthew had to insist we head back to shore before the sunset.

Pap strolled down to the beach to meet us. He needed the boat to check and clean the kelp from his nets one last time while it was still light. "Some wonderful fine rowing, Patience," he said.

Later, the three of us sat with our backs pressed against the weather-beaten cabin. Pap's elbows rested on his bent knees, his clasped hands in front of him. He had his felt brown hat pulled down around his forehead against the glare of the setting sun. He lit his pipe. The smoke floated away from his tanned face and upward to heaven. I sat as close as I could to him and in the same position. I pretended I was smoking a curved pipe too. Matthew sat with his legs straight out in front of him throwing rocks towards the water. Life could only be better if Nan were here.

Which story would I ask Pap to tell me this evening? Would I ask him to tell me about his hunting trips in the wilderness, tall tales about the local folks or some ghost story about one of our dead relatives? Whichever one I chose, I knew the ending would be different – it always was.

I puffed on my make-believe pipe. "I sure would like to hear the story about great-grand," I said, blowing my pretend smoke away from his face.

"It's a perfect story before bedtime," Matthew said.

My Favourite Place

Pap squinted under his felt hat. He removed the pipe from his lips with his left hand and held it in front of his knees. Deep breath. Eyes somewhere towards the horizon. He was so focused I expected to see his dear departed mother coming in sight at any moment. "I will never forget da night me mother died. It was one a dose pitch black nights. Da wind was howling like a mad dog. Fer no reason in particular, I was lonesome – queer feelings in me stomach. I was sure I would be hearing some bad news. Went to bed about midnight. Dis weary feeling wouldn't go away. I tossed and turned." Pap puffed hard on his pipe. Eyes still squinting.

"About two o'clock in da morning – couldn't sleep a wink – got up. Went in da kitchen and put some wood in da stove."

He lowered his voice. "Suddenly, it was like time had stopped. A strange stillness comed over da room. I could feel da goose bumps up and down me body. Me hair stuck straight up on da back of me neck. A lady entered da room. She didn't walk in da door but floated right through it. Dis really got me attention."

Other than Pap's words, all I could hear were the waves lapping on the beach.

"Her ghostlike figure floated o'er towards me. She sat on da chair facing me. I realized her face was da sweet face of me dear mother – God bless her soul. She held out her cold hand to me. 'Don't be afraid, me son. God called me home. I's in heaven,' she said. Then she kissed me. Never before in me life was me mother's kiss so cold. And she faded away – just like dat." He snapped his fingers sharply. Matthew and I both jumped.

My Favourite Place

The lights across the bay came on one by one. We watched until Nan's light came on, too.

Pap put his hands back on his knees. "I knew me dear sweet mother was no longer with us. Within fifteen minutes me brother, William, comed to tell me Mother passed away at two o'clock." He put his pipe back in his mouth and inhaled deeply.

The sun had almost set and surrounded by silence and the sweet smell of tobacco I was lost in Pap's story.

"BOO!"

My heart nearly left my body. All thoughts of great-grandmother disappeared.

I grabbed a handful of fresh fish guts and chased after Matthew. He was going to get his face washed good!

CHAPTER 11

A Stranger at Our Door

"Now, who could dat be dis hour in da day knocking on me door?" said Nan, walking to the porch. It had to be a stranger. Anyone living in Dearing Bay would have walked right on in.

I stopped colouring and followed Nan, clinging to her skirt. It was a pale young man with lifeless eyes. He leaned a large package against the house. "I'm sell-selling pic-pictures. W-would y-y-you like to s-see 'em?" His hands shook and his brow gleamed with sweat.

"Would you like a drop a tea, sir?" said Nan. "It's dinner time and all." Nan fed anyone who dropped by.

Darn it. Why couldn't she feed him after we seen his pictures?

"You going to join us, Patience?"

"No thanks, Nan." The truth was, sitting across the table from the stranger didn't lend itself to what I had in mind. Nan told me staring at people was rude so I didn't want to get caught sizing up our guest.

"Sit yurself in now, sir and eat up 'cause you must be hungry." Nan poured tea, first for him, then for herself.

The nameless dark-haired man sat himself down at our table and crossed himself. Nan said grace.

A Stranger at Our Door

I studied the stranger's greasy hair. Dandruff clung to the crown of his head and decorated the collar of his jacket. The elbows of the wrinkled brown tweed had patches on top of patches. The cuffs on his dark brown pants rode midway up his hairless lily-white legs. His socks, down around his ankles, were well-mended, and without elastic. He crossed his ankles and tucked them under his chair, exposing holes in the soles of his scuffed shoes. He must have slept in his clothes, and gone without washing them for days.

Our stranger devoured three thick slices of homemade white bread covered with rhubarb pickles, three chunks of cheddar cheese, two slices of fresh-from-the-oven molasses raisin bread, a full tin of corn beef and a large serving of sailor's duff. He followed all that with a slab of fruit cake, two bowls of fruit cocktail and two cups of strong tea with condensed milk and white sugar. He bolted every mouthful down like Sam, Hilda Mae's farm dog. I swear, I had never seen anyone eat so much in such a short time. And still he reached for more.

Nan, sipping her hot tea and nibbling on a small piece of fruit cake, encouraged him to make up his meal.

They didn't converse.

Where was the food going inside this skinny man? I let my imagination run wild. I saw him explode. Pieces of our stranger all over Nan's white ceiling. And Pap had just finished repainting it yesterday. Meat, fruitcake, bread and cheese peppered the walls, the windows, the cupboards, the table. Sailor duff and fruit all over Nan's hair and face. His dandruff head in her apron. My tummy rolled.

"I could make another pot of tea," said Nan, "if you would like more."

I pictured him burping and farting. The walls turning brown, the same colour as his clothes. I held my nose. Nan kept looking at me. She was having trouble keeping her composure. Burp. Belch. A short fart. A long, screeching fart.

Nan finally got annoyed. "Patience, what is you laughing at?"

A hot flush rolled up from my neck to my face.

Nan gave me her knowing look, and turned her attention back to her guest. "Now, let me see yur pictures, me son."

The salesman carefully lifted each print out of the carton and handed it to Nan. She studied each one with equal consideration. "Dey is very nice, sir. How much is dem?"

"Da small ones is one dollar. Da big ones is three dollars," he said. Amazingly, he was no longer nervous.

"Da one of 'Christ on da Cross' is some nice." She held it up towards the wall for a better look. "So tis da 'Last Supper'."

"I like this one best of all," I said. It was a picture of a fluffy, white cat sitting next to a goldfish bowl. Maybe Nan would get it for me. I had a perfect spot for it in my bedroom.

"I'll take da three of dem sir," she said, pulling five dollars out of her apron pocket and handing it to the salesman.

"Thank-you, ma'am," he said. "Thank-you very much, indeed."

Was this the same man who came to our door an hour ago? Strangely, his shoddy outer appearance didn't seem to matter anymore. He was a different person. Nan's knack of making people feel good had worked on our stranger.

Nan reached out and shook his hand. "Yur very welcome, me son," she said.

Our stranger, head held high, walked towards the door. He turned towards Nan and said, "God bless you, ma'am." His voice, although strong, shook with feeling.

"Oh. And you too, sir," said Nan. She seemed taken back by his gratitude.

Nan tidied up the kitchen, lost in her thoughts. Was she reflecting on her day with the stranger or was she disappointed in my bad manners? I dared not say a word. I was feeling ashamed and hoped she wouldn't scold me. How many times would I have to be told not to be rude before I learned my lesson? I promised myself I would be kind, more like Nan, if she let me off just this time.

Nan didn't say a word until all the dishes were put away. "Patience, help me put up da pictures before Tom and Matthew gits home from da woods," she said, briskly drying her hands on her apron. "Don't want Tom taking nar hammer tonight, to me freshly painted walls. Dat's fer sure."

CHAPTER 12

Our Annual Valentine Box

"Children, tis St. Valentine's Day tomorrow," said Nan, soapy dish water up to her elbows, and eyes dancing. "I picked up some nice box at da store today. Will be lovely when we's done with it."

Each year under Nan's guidance, we turned an ordinary cardboard box into a beautiful piece of artwork. I was almost certain that Matthew or I was always chosen to decorate the valentine box because Nan secretly volunteered her services.

While Matthew and I finished off supper Pap sat by the old Franklin stove having a smoke and a mug of tea. The tea kettle simmered away. "Come on, eat your figgy duff, Patience. Matthew, bring me the rest of da dirty dishes," said Nan. "Leave da milk on da table." We didn't have real glue for the box so we would need the condensed milk as a substitute.

Minutes later, there wasn't a dirty dish in sight. Nan bustled around. "Matthew, git da valentines and da tissue paper sitting on me trunk. Patience, git da scissors in me sewing basket and da brown wrapping paper in da cupboard." Nan ordered valentines from the catalogue in early fall. Only store-bought cards would do for this occasion. Lucky Matthew and me –

the only children in school who didn't have to make do with brown paper valentines.

We sat around the table in our cozy kitchen. The only light in the house was a glow from the kerosene oil lamp and a reflection on the wall from the flames in the open stove. Nan laughed and giggled like a girl as we worked. "Dis year we will make da best one ever."

"You say that every year," I said.

Nan hovered over us as we carefully snipped the lacy hearts. Once satisfied we weren't going to get wild with the scissors she moved on to the box. She ironed the brown wrapping paper and then pasted it on the box. While it was drying she cut hearts out of red tissue paper left over from Christmas. Soon she was helping us finish cutting out the store-bought valentines, unmindful of the trimmings falling on her normally immaculate floors. For the first time, she let Matthew make the slit in the top. I got to paste on the final heart.

"Tom, come and see da box," she said.

"Rose, tis da best one ever," said Pap, teasing Nan and winking at Matthew and me.

On Valentine's Day Matthew and I were out of bed at the crack of dawn. Other than Christmas and Easter, it was the only time we could even hope for a break from regular school work.

"I hope Mr. Jake is in a good mood," Matthew said. Mr. Jake came in December after our old teacher, Miss Jones, had passed away in her sleep.

"I can't wait to be rid of Mr. Jake for good," I said.

Typical for mid-February in Newfoundland, frosty snow covered every track and path in sight. "Pull your toque down over your ears, Patience," said Nan. I stepped out into the cold morning air with my bookbag on my back and the valentine box carefully held in my arms. Pap helped me on with my snowshoes and I followed after Matthew.

"Patience, da snow is deep. You should let Matthew carry da box," Pap called after us.

"It's my turn," I yelled back. I knew I should listen to Pap but I was too impatient to pay any mind.

We had not walked more than fifty feet when I managed to cross one of my snowshoes over the other and took a dive headfirst into a snowbank. The weight of my body flattened our pretty decorated box. I tried to get back on my feet but the harder I worked the deeper I sunk in the snow.

I could hear Matthew laughing hysterically. If the situation was reversed I would have laughed too. But the snow was stinging the insides of my wrists and sticking to my eyebrows and hair. I slapped the squished valentine box with my one free hand and it rolled over and over on the snow before it stopped. I began to cry.

Matthew, trying to suppress his laughter, came to my rescue. He helped me back on my feet and brushed the snow from my face and clothes.

"Don't cry, Patience. I can fix da darn 'ole valentine box."

Luckily, Nan had wrapped it in plastic so it didn't get damaged from the snow. And true to his word, in a few minutes Matthew had the box looking like new. "Want me to carry it for you?"

I sniffed. "Okay."

Our Annual Valentine Box

At the schoolhouse the children greeted us. Matthew removed the plastic from our beautiful valentine box and set it on Mr. Jake's desk.

"It's more beautiful then last year," said Becky Sanders, the oldest girl in the school.

"Yes, tis," said Matthew.

I held my breath, hoping Matthew wouldn't tell about my face dive.

Mr. Jake rang the school bell sharply at nine. Everyone took their seats. "Drop your valentines in the box starting with the first row. If I hear anything from anyone of you today, we won't be celebrating Valentine's Day," he said. "Instead you will be writing a hundred lines each."

Jake the Snake. I looked at Matthew. I could tell he was thinking the same thing.

The morning and early afternoon dragged on and on. We were like little angels, not wanting to vex Mr. Jake. At last it was two o'clock!

"Well now, if only you acted like this every day," said Mr. Jake. I hated his heartless eyes. "Come up to my desk when I call your name." There was no feeling in his words. "David Edwards."

My card to David was special. It was the biggest one in the box – a teddy bear with a big red heart which read, 'For my Very Best Friend'.

"Hilda Mae Murphy."

I gave her an appropriate one, a fat skunk that said, 'You stink on Valentine's Day'. I didn't want to give her one but Nan said I wasn't allowed to leave out anyone.

"Matthew Dearing."

I looked over his shoulder. It was a picture of a tall cowboy on a horse which read, 'Be Mine'. Who was it from?

"Patience Dearing."

Mine was a picture of a cupid which read, 'I'm Patient for You on Valentine's Day', signed 'Guess Who'.

All our names had gotten called several times and the box was almost empty. I was sitting on the edge of my chair like most of the others. The last name called got to keep the valentine box. It would be nice to take it home just once.

Mr. Jake reached into the box. "Becky Sanders," he said, and ripped open the envelope. None of us could believe our eyes. How dare Mr. Jake open Becky's valentine. "It reads, 'My love is yours forever'," he scoffed. "And it's from Matthew Dearing." Mr. Jake slapped Becky's card back in the box and tossed it to her. He looked around the room with his stone-cold eyes, and smiled his dead smile.

Matthew's face turned as red as a boiled lobster.

Becky met Matthew's eyes. "Thank-you," she said calmly.

"Nan, Matthew likes Becky Sanders," I said, that evening. "You should had seen how red he turned when Mr. Jake blabbed to the class."

Nan's dark eyes twinkled and her throaty laughter filled the room. "Becky is a fine girl," she said.

"I bet he had her valentine glued to the bottom of the box so she would be last," I said, needling him for laughing at me this morning.

"Oh, Patience, you are some silly," said Matthew, but he blushed all over again.

That night I reflected on the events of the day. Only a few things kept it from being perfect – my eagerness to carry the valentine box and Mr. Jake. I got out of my bed and got down on my knees. "Bless Matthew for saving the day," I prayed. "And Lord, if you're listening, could you help me live up to my name – however I got it. And God, please make Mr. Jake go away."

CHAPTER 13

My Spotted Friend

"SHELIA HAD HER LAMBS last night," Pap said. "Three of dem – a white one, a black one and a spotted one."

I couldn't wait to see them and fell in love with the black-and-white spotted lamb as soon as I laid eyes on her. She was the smallest of the three and as cute as a cuddly puppy. Matthew and I took turns holding all three of them, petting their faces and ears. Only the spotted one responded to our touch. Her brothers preferred to be left alone. "Let's call her Spot." I had never seen a spotted sheep before.

"Spot is a good name for a dog," said Matthew. "Might be okay for a male, but for a ewe – don't think so."

"Oh, poppycock." I had heard the parson's wife use the word one day when she wasn't in agreement with something. "Spot is a perfectly good name for boy lambs and girl lambs." I had my legs shoulder-width apart and my hands at my waist. "Why do people make stupid rules?"

"Have it your way, Patience. But when people make fun, remember I told you so."

All the time I petted my new friend Pap's words echoed through my head. *Don't treat the animals like pets, they are raised for food.* We lived on a small farm.

My Spotted Friend

We kept cows and pigs for meat; chickens and ducks for eggs and poultry; horses and dogs for transportation; and lambs mostly for wool. Just maybe, Spot would be kept for wool.

Nan stopped by on her way to her vegetable garden where every year, she grew potatoes, turnip, cabbage, carrots and beets. "Patience, don't get too attached to dat lamb," she said. She had seen me cry myself to sleep too many times over a beloved pet who had gone to pet heaven so we could eat meat during the winter. I kissed Spot on her wee black nose. There was no guarantee that she would be spared.

For the first month, Shelia and her babies spent most of their time in the barnyard. For some reason, Shelia had more patience with Spot than with her other lambs and allowed her more time to suck. Soon though, Spot was running with her brothers. Matthew and I visited the sheep every day and often Spot would prance right up and nuzzle her nose in my hand. I'd scratch her ears and face.

When spring turned into summer sheep, horses, goats and cows roamed wild, grazing on the green pastures surrounding our little village. It was time for Spot to have her freedom for the first time. Shelia, Roxanne, Myrtle, Bernard, Dief and Spot's father, Smallwood, headed toward the lush grass along the water edge. I clung to Spot's neck. I didn't want my woolly friend to leave.

"You must let her join da others," said Pap.

I kissed Spot's head and scratched her ears one last time. "Off you go." Spot raced along and joined her brothers with one final glance back before she headed over the hill. Would she remember me when she came home?

Summer slipped into September. I kept my eyes peeled to the north. Any day the sheep would be coming home for winter. One afternoon, I heard baaaing in the distance and raced to the top of the hill. Spot stuck out in the middle of the herd. She was much bigger, much woollier and no longer a baby. "Spot, over here."

Spot lifted her head and tilted an ear. She hadn't forgotten me. I could feel it in my heart and I knew by the way she looked at me. Then she ran to me and nuzzled her face into my hand. She closed her eyes when I scratched her ears.

I got to play with Spot all winter and before I knew it, it was spring and time to shear the sheep. Spot kicked and wiggled. She didn't like what we were doing to her one little bit. "Hold her head, Patience," said Nan. "Matthew, her legs – a bit tighter. David, hand me da shears."

Nan had already cropped the rest of the herd. Spot was her last. Soon a heap of black and white wool lay on the grass in front of Nan's feet. Nan scooped it into piles and then stuffed it into a potato sack. "I don't know what use I'd have fer dat spotted wool," she said. "Couldn't follow nar pattern with it, dat's fer sure."

Spot's dark eyes looked too big for her face now that she was stripped of her wool. Nan, who wasn't a skillful shearer and only did it because she had to, had clipped Spot too close in places and exposed patches of skin. Spot reminded me of the time Mr. Edwards gave David a brushcut with dull clippers. Spot looked sad without wool. "Nan, does shearing hurt the sheep?"

"My goodness – no," she said impatiently. I knew she didn't want me to get started. Sometimes I drove her crazy with my questions about the animals.

"Spot will be all woolly again when she comes home in the fall," Matthew said.

He was right. That fall when the sheep came home Spot's coat was thicker than ever. Unfortunately fall was also butchering season.

I was drawing pictures of my favourite animals at the kitchen table one crisp October morning. Just yesterday, I had heard Nan and Pap talking. Nan said there were only two jars of lamb left. Pap's response was that lamb stew sure was good on a cold winter's night. This morning Nan had washed three dozen jars. They were sitting upside down on the kitchen table next to the best picture of Spot I had ever done.

Suddenly David barged in, out of breath. "Patience! Come quickly, Spot is on her way to heaven."

My heart pounded against my chest. I had to save Spot. But how?

I ran outside on shaky legs. There was no time for tears. Besides, I was too shocked to cry. There was Pap, gun in one hand, leading Spot behind the barn.

"Spot!"

She lifted her head and looked my way. She bleated, and I knew she was begging me to help her.

I had a dramatic, fleeting notion of taking the bullet myself but Nan held me back. "No Pap," I cried, but it was too late. The barnyard was already echoing with the sound of a single gunshot.

CHAPTER 14

Kingsley

NAN HAD HAD IT WITH GWEN. "I's going to git one of me good hens to nest on the duck eggs dis time," she said. "Dis will be me only chance at saving a complete flock."

Gwen, our duck, had a tendency to nest in secret places. Only when she came home with a dozen or so babies behind her did we know what she was up to. Out of all those babies, only one or two lived. The others simply disappeared. All Gwen's fault, according to Nan.

Nan spent a great deal of time watching her favourite hen nesting patiently on green eggs that were much bigger than her own. She was waiting to see the first signs of life. "Today I's going to test one of dem eggs," she said. "Dat hen's been sitting long enough."

Nan took an egg from under the hen and tapped it lightly with a stick. The eggshell split in half and a rotten mixture of yellow and white splattered on her shoes.

She tried another and a dead baby duck fell to the ground. Another – nothing. Soon all the eggs were broken. Nan carried the broody hen from her nest and threw her into the pond. "Back to laying fer you, me lady," she said, taking her disappointment out on the poor hen. It wasn't the hen's fault that the ducks didn't hatch. Wings flapping and squawking, she tried to return to her nest. Nan, a fir bough in hand, chased the hen outside again. "Git away. Go on. Git."

"Nan! Look – one is alive," I said, pointing to a black-and-yellow movement on the sawdust floor. One wet wing moved. Its eyes were tightly sealed, the world around it a complete mystery.

Nan fell to her knees. She gently picked up the tiny creature, dried it off and placed it inside her dress, next to her warm bosom. "You precious little thing," she said.

Nan's determination to save the little duckling kept her up all night. "I can't come to bed," she called to Pap from her rocking chair by the living room window. "Kingsley is warm and cosy. He is sleeping next to me heart."

By morning Kingsley was able to stand on his own. Nan fed him a few breadcrumbs from her hand. She carried him around for the rest of the day inside her dress. That night he slept in a box with straw, near the kitchen stove.

Several weeks passed by and Kingsley became stronger and stronger. He followed us like a dog around the kitchen. He even came to the door to greet us. Matthew and I liked having a duck in the house. It gave us something different to talk about. Then one day, Nan said, "Tomorrow Kingsley joins da other ducks in da pond."

It was beautiful outside. The ducks were swimming and diving. Nan led Kingsley down to the pond. She thought he would just dive in and get on with it. Much to her surprise and disappointment, the little fellow didn't think he was a duck. He seemed scared to death of water. She tried to persuade him to swim. But no matter how often she put him in the water, Kingsley quacked and quacked and flapped his wings desperately until he was safely back on shore.

Two of the ducks waddled up the bank towards Kingsley. He ran in the opposite direction, wings flapping, as fast as his legs could carry him. Soon he was airborne. But not for long. He flew into Nan's sheets, hanging on the clothesline, and crashed to the ground. "Guess he's afraid of ducks," I said.

"What a situation I have meself in," Nan said. "Da duck is too big and too messy to stay inside. I don't know what I's going to do with him."

In desperation, she took him over to the chicken yard. He didn't want to be there either. Every time she tried to leave him behind, he followed her. "Kingsley, you can't live in da house no more. You either live with da ducks in da pond or da chickens here." Kingsley, of course, wanted to be with us so Nan made the decision. The chicken coop would be Kingsley's new home.

Poor Kingsley. He became the laughing stock of our village – a duck raised by humans, who lived in a chicken coop and afraid of his own kind, and water. Every day, while the chickens roamed, Kingsley came to visit. He expected to come on inside and eat with us. He particularly didn't like being sent back to the chicken coop at night.

One afternoon, David and I were watching the ducks splashing in the pond. Kingsley was feeding with the chickens on the banks. "It isn't right for Kingsley to spend his entire life afraid of water," said David. "After all, he's a duck."

"Let's teach him how to swim," I said.

"Kingsley," I called. He waddled over to me and I lifted him up and placed him in Nan's large laundry tub filled with water. Quacking, he paddled his little legs much too fast and frenziedly flapped his wings. Within a few seconds, he was out of the water, falling headfirst over the side of the tub. He ran, neck straight out, toward Nan who was sitting on the steps to the house. "Catch him, Nan."

"Keep your hands under his body," said Nan. "Perhaps he's scared of drowning." David and I both laughed at the thought.

After feeding Kingsley a piece of bread to settle him down, I held him with both hands in the water, while David fed him by hand. Next, David dropped a piece of bread in the pan. Kingsley snapped it up as soon as it hit the water. "Good boy, Kingsley," I said.

David and I worked with Kingsley every day until he got used to floating and moving on his own. "I think we should try him in the duck pond," said David.

We waited until all of the other ducks were out of sight before we waded into the water. I took Kingsley out from under my arm and put him down gently on the calm water. "Don't be afraid, Kingsley. We'll stay close so you won't drown," I said. David and I giggled. Kingsley remained calm. David fed him bread, moving it farther away, bit by bit. But Kingsley refused to go more than two feet away from us. When David and I walked out of the water, Kingsley followed. "Enough for today. Tomorrow we'll do it all over again. Brave Kingsley."

One day, several months after Kingsley finally took to swimming, Matthew and I were walking home alone from school. "Matthew, your Mom and Daddy is my Nan and Pap," I said. Lately, I had found myself pondering this situation. Something just didn't add up.

Matthew shrugged his shoulders. He threw a stone at an old tin can on the beach. "It's all the same, isn't it?" he said.

"Not really. The way I figure it, you and I are not brother and sister." I held my breath, hoping for a reaction.

But all Matthew said was, "We grew up like brother and sister. That's what counts, isn't it?" Then he threw another stone. *Zing*. A tin can bounced in the air.

"Yeah, but aren't you even curious... Or do you already know something?" Matthew continued pitching stones. "I just want to know who I am."

Slob, a heavy sludge of sea ice, was forming in places around the bay. The cold air stung my nose. I walked as slowly as I could, though, hoping Matthew would talk to me about Nan and Pap. But he wasn't even listening. He was pointing to the ducks down the beach. "I can't see Kingsley with the other ducks," he said.

I hadn't even noticed that Kingsley hadn't come to greet us. Every day he left the water and the other ducks behind to follow us home. Something was wrong.

Kingsley

We checked the area where the ducks had gathered. Kingsley was nowhere to be seen. I ran into the yard calling for Nan.

"He left with dem others dis morning," Nan said, coming up from the woodhouse with an armful of wood. "Hope he's not caught in the slob somewhere." The temperature was below freezing. It wouldn't be long before the salt water and all of its goodies would be off limits to the ducks for another season. "Hurry, we must find Kingsley 'fore dark," she said. "Go grab da flashlight, Matthew."

The orange sun was close to saying goodnight to the world for another day by the time Nan had pulled on her warm winter coat and high rubber boots.

"Go look in da chicken coop, Patience," Nan said. "Matthew, you check in da duck house. I'll look in da yard."

The rest of the ducks were finding their way back home for the night but neither Matthew or I had any other news for Nan.

"Let's take a gander down da beach," said Nan.

We followed the beach around the point for quite some distance. No luck.

"I dare say Kingsley couldn't keep up with da others, just slow coming home. He isn't much of a duck at da best of times," Nan said.

I sensed she was making conversation to keep us calm. The wind was stronger around the point and blowing in from the open ocean. The temperature was dropping by the minute and my ears and forehead were stinging from the cold. Matthew was jumping around trying to keep warm. There was no doubt that Kingsley would be in deep trouble if we were unable to find him. Likely the bay would be frozen over by morning.

By now the sun had gone down completely and the moon was rising over the ocean. We scanned the beach and shoreline with our flashlight.

"We should go back," Nan said. I doubt if Kingsley would swim dis far. Perhaps he made hes way back home by now."

My gut told me we would not find Kingsley at home. "Please Nan, let Matthew and me go around the next cove. You could wait here fer us," I said. "Please, Nan." Tears stung my eyes.

Nan reluctantly handed over the flashlight. "Don't waste time or we'll all catch our deaths."

Matthew and I scrambled along the familiar rocks calling and calling until our throats were raw. "You damn duck!" I finally screamed.

"Hope Mom didn't hear you say the 'd' word," Matthew said.

"If she did it's all Kingsley's fault," I said. I knew we'd have to turn back soon. Where was that damn duck?

Then I heard something.

"Did you hear that?"

Matthew listened intently for a few seconds. "The wind is playing tricks on you," he said.

"Kingsley," I yelled.

Quack!

Matthew heard it this time too. We both ran towards the sound, Matthew aiming the light towards the water.

There was Kingsley, caught in the slob.

"Nan! Over here. Kingsley is over here," I yelled.

"How in da world am I going to free him," Nan said, running up to us. She hesitated a minute and stepped into the water and waded out to the top of her rubber boots.

I prayed she wouldn't slip.

"I can't reach him," she said. "Da water is too deep."

I found a long, pointed stick and handed it to her. "Can you break up the ice around him with this?"

Nan picked and picked at the slob. It seemed to take forever until Kingsley was free. He swam to Nan and followed her ashore. "If I weren't so happy to see you, I would ring yur bloody neck," she said. Matthew and I pretended to be shocked at Nan's words. Kingsley didn't seem to mind being scolded. He quacked a few times and snuggled into Nan's arms.

"Poor Kingsley doesn't realize he's a duck," I said.

"He doesn't know who he is," said Matthew.

And neither did I.

CHAPTER 15

The Price of Carelessness

"You call that a horse," said Matthew. "It looks like a camel." He held my drawings in front of him. "Is that a dog?"

I picked up his pictures off the kitchen table. "No sane Newfoundlander would recognize these fish."

"I don't want to draw any more," said Matthew. "Let's clean up this mess before Mom comes in."

Nan and Pap were down at the beach, chopping frozen sand for the chickens. Matthew and I were alone. "Hilda Mae and I got into it again at school today," I said, carefully stacking my drawings.

"So, what's new? You and Hilda Mae are always into it."

"Today she said something really strange. She asked why I lived with Nan and Pap, instead of my real parents."

I slowly put my crayons into the box. Finally, Matthew asked me what I said.

"So, what did you say?"

"What do you think I said? I told her to mind her own business."

Matthew reached for the crayon box and I turned to face him across the kitchen table.

"She said it in front of all of the kids. Later, they were whispering in little groups. I know they were talking about me."

I crossed my arms in front of me. I had to know. "Matthew, why do I live with Nan and Pap?"

Matthew leaned towards me. He did know something! Finally, someone was going to tell me the truth.

"Matthew! Patience!"

We ran to the window. Matthew opened it to hear what Nan was saying. "Da chickens laid dir first egg."

Outside, Nan held the egg out to us, handling it as carefully as a gold nugget. Not only was it our first egg of the season, it was the only egg in the entire village. For months, Nan had hauled sand from the beach to the hen house, ever since she could dig it along the frozen shoreline. Sand, she firmly believed, was the key ingredient to help chickens shell their eggs.

"I get to eat it! I get to eat it!" sang Matthew.

"You had the first one last year," I said.

"Share or nar one of you will git a bite to put inside yur mouths," Nan said.

We both shut up. We knew she was serious.

Later, the aroma of fresh frying egg filled the air. Nan served it with home-made bread and store-bought butter.

Matthew and I pushed our plates towards her.

"Matthew, cut it in half." said Nan. "And, remember if your half is bigger than Patience's, you will have to switch plates with her."

Matthew sliced the egg into two precisely equal pieces. We both savoured every mouthful, regretting the last bite.

The Price of Carelessness

By the time the snow and ice had disappeared the chickens were laying more eggs than we could use. Some were nesting. This pleased Nan. Her flock of one hundred would soon be bigger. She preferred chickens over all of the animals on the farm, especially good laying hens with big bushy topknots.

Saturday, after finishing our chores, Matthew and I were digging worms in a pile of horse manure near the barn. "Matthew, what were you going to tell me that day when Nan got her first egg?" I said. I picked up a wiggling earth worm and dropped it in the rusty tin can.

"Oh that." said Matthew. "I've been meaning to tell you. But everytime I think about it, Mom or Dad is around." He glanced down the path. "They'd kill me if they knew I looked in their trunk."

"Trunk?" I dropped my stick. "What does the trunk have to do with it?"

"Mom keeps a picture of a woman in her trunk," he said. "One day I was playing on the ladder. I could see Mom in her room. Crying. She had a snapshot in her hands. Matthew turned over a rotten log. It was crawling with worms. One by one he picked them up. "She kissed the picture before she put it back."

"And you looked in the trunk?" I said.

"I knew I shouldn't," he said. "But that's not the best part." Worms were wiggling through his fingers. "The woman in the picture reminds me of someone. But I don't know who. Strange, eh?"

"Very strange."

"Let's go fishing," said Matthew. Already he had seemed to have put behind him what he just told me.

But I thought of nothing else. Who was the woman in the picture?

We fished for a few hours off the rocks in front of our house. "Nothing much is biting today," Matthew said. He'd refused to talk anymore about the woman.

"I'm going to try one more big, juicy red earth worm," I said. "And if I don't get a bite, I'm going inside to eat." I swung my bamboo pole back over my shoulder and snapped it forward. My line went out quite a distance. I watched the cork float and float. Not a single nibble.

"I've had enough of this," said Matthew. He wrapped his fishing line around the top of his pole, hook firmly affixed to the other end. Just like Pap showed him.

"You're right," I said. "Wait until I get my line in. I'm famished." We placed our bamboo poles on top of the five-foot high picket fence. Pap insisted that we store our fishing gear that way.

"Nar fish today," Nan said when we got home. "Want a chicken sandwich?"

Matthew and I bolted down one each. I reached for a second and piercing squawks stopped me dead. Everyone dashed outside. One of Nan's favourite chickens was flying all over the place.

The hen flapped towards me and was brought up suddenly, her head yanked back over her body. Flapping and squawking, she tore in the opposite direction until she ran out of line. Oh my God, I had forgotten to remove the worm from my hook before I went inside. The poor hen had swallowed it, thinking it was an easy bite of food.

The Price of Carelessness

Pap caught the panicking hen and held her wings. "Rose, she has swallowed da hook completely," he said. "Not much I can do."

Nan, who seldom weeped, wiped at her cheeks. "Me best laying hen," she cried. "Patience." She choked on her words. "You must be more careful with yur hooks."

Pap took the chicken over to the chopping block. "Matthew, git me me axe, son?"

I stood there with half a chicken sandwich still in my hand. "What are you going to do with her?" I said.

"Put da poor t'ing out of her punishment," Pap said.

I could not bear to watch. I ran straight to my bedroom and covered up my head, hands tightly held to my ears. The chop of the axe echoed through the open window and the squawking stopped.

That night, I tossed and turned, unable to sleep. Pap came in and sat beside me, stroking my head. "Der is nothing worst den carelessness, dat's fer sure," he said.

CHAPTER 16

The Secret

"PATIENCE, WAKE UP. Wake up, child."

I bolted upright in the cabin bunk. My heart was racing and my pyjamas were glued to my sweaty body. I pushed my head into Pap's chest and sobbed. I was so lonely.

"It's just a nightmare, Patience," he said. "Pap is here now – everything will be all right." He stroked my damp hair. "Hush. Hush. Go back to sleep, darling."

Lately, the dream was more frequent – at least once a week. A woman. A man. Reaching out to me. I reach for them. There's a powerful feeling of love and belonging. Our fingers nearly touch. Then they pull away and are gone. Why do I wake up with my heart breaking?

I finally fell back to sleep trying to understand what the dream could possibly mean.

"Let's cook breakfast outside," said Pap. "Tis such a wonderful morning."

It was a nice treat to not have Pap rush off and check his nets first thing. I had lots on my mind and I could do with the company. Matthew and Nan hadn't come this time so Pap and I had the cabin all to ourselves for the weekend.

"Bad dream again last night, eh," said Pap, cutting strips off the bacon slab.

The Secret

"Yeah," I said. A million questions rushed through my head. I'd thought of speaking to Nan before we left. Considering what Matthew had told me, I just couldn't bring myself to do it. Besides, I didn't want to get him in trouble over the picture in the trunk. "I think I know why ... The bad dreams – why I get them."

Pap took off his hat, scratched his head, put it back on before he spoke. He stroked his chin. "You do."

"I believe it has to do with my real Mom and Dad. Lately, I think about them a lot. Like who they are and why we don't talk about them." The words were coming easier than I would have thought possible. I told him about what Hilda Mae had said. Leaving Matthew out of it, I told him about Nan crying over a picture of a woman she kept in her trunk.

Pap's deep blue eyes turned a few shades paler. He wiped his eye, blaming the tear on a piece of dirt. He coughed and tried to regain his composure.

"Patience, me darling, I figgered dat was on yur mind." Pap wiped his fingers over his lips. "Now dat you brought it up...."

First, Pap told me about my father. His name was Patrick. He and Mom had been married only two months when he and his two brothers left for the Labrador Coast. Mom begged him not to go. She was expecting me and was certain she would never see him again. Dad didn't pay any attention to her – said his mother said the same thing, every time his own father went fishing.

Dad's boat, *The Optimist*, went down one stormy night, swells sixty feet high. All hands drowned. Their bodies were never found.

"Eh, Patience, me love, you remind me of Patrick at times," Pap said. "Once he got something in his head, God hisself couldn't change his mind."

"My stubborn streak," I said.

"You got a mind of yur own – jest like yur Daddy," said Pap. He winked at me.

Pap said Mom wept for a week or more after she heard. After that she grieved in silence for the longest time, didn't say anything to anyone. Then one day Mom headed down around the cove. Pap, following out of concern, saw her fall to her knees in the meadow. Damn you, Patrick, she screamed. Why did you leave me?

"Dat night at da supper table – your Mother – she made a strange request of your Nan and me," said Pap. "Still don't understand her reason. Right to dis day, I don't."

I stared at Pap. "Request?"

"Elizabeth made us swear we would never mention Patrick ever again," said Pap. "Pretend he was never born, she said."

"What happened to my mother?" I said.

Pap broke four eggs into the sizzling bacon grease. "Haven't you heard plenty for one day?"

I grabbed Pap's hand. "I need to know everything."

Apparently Mom never spoke of Dad again. Nan and Pap never mentioned my father in front of her. Mom did her best at getting on with her life. Then, I came along and her life was full again.

"Your mother was some proud of you," said Pap. "Showed you off at Sunday school. Fixed yur hair, made pretty clothes fer you. She loved you all right." I couldn't help smiling. Pap smiled back. I think he was glad to finally be talking about this.

"Elizabeth was young, you know. Restless at times. Other den you – not a lot fer her in da bay. She wanted a paying job." Pap turned the bread in the frying pan.

The Canadian Armed Forces came to the bay, looking for recruits. With Nan and Pap's encouragement Mom signed up for two years in nursing at St. John's. She came home every chance she got. After graduation, she accepted a job in England. She had to get situated before I could join her. Soon though, a letter arrived telling Nan and Pap that Mom was catching a ride on a cargo ship. She'd be home in a few weeks and then she'd be taking me back to England.

Pap paused for a very long time. "Elizabeth didn't make it home," he said finally. Tears filled his eyes. "Another rough night on da Labrador Coast, swells as high as da night yur father's ship when down." He coughed and rubbed his eyes. "Da ship, all da poor ole souls, never seen again. Including yur poor mother, me darling."

My feelings were mixed. I was relieved to finally know who I was but how could I make Pap's hurt go away?

I couldn't.

"One more bit, you should know, Patience," he said, his breakfast hardly touched.

A message was found in Mother's belongings that were sent back from England. It simply said: "Mom and Dad, if something happens to me, raise Patience as your own. Tell her about Patrick and me, only if she asks. Her Daddy and I will always be with her, no matter what. Elizabeth, your loving daughter."

"Dats yur big secret, Patience, me love." We both cried and held each other. I wasn't sure if he was comforting me or I was comforting him. It was noon before Pap checked his nets.

That evening Pap and I were sitting by the campfire. The last glimmer of the golden orange sun was about to slip out of sight. "Pap, you are my best grown-up friend in the whole wide world."

"I am? Well, let me tell you dat you is me best young girl friend in da whole wide world. Now, don't tell Nan or she will be jealous."

"Pap, I am glad I live with you and Nan and Matthew," I said. "I'm the luckiest girl in Dearing Bay." I poked at the coals making sparks fly all around us. "Just the same, I wish my Mom and Dad were alive."

"Nan and me too. Matthew – well, he was young and don't remember. Your uncles don't say much, but dey was shook up. Dere only sister, God rest her soul. Didn't think we'd ever git over it. Even got mad at God fer taking her. Still git king size goose bumps, head to toe, knowing her body is somewhere on dat ocean floor."

Pap stood up and threw the last of his tea on the fire. "But tis not da nature of the Labrador seas to give up its dead."

That night I dreamed a gentle summer breeze was blowing off the water. Robins flaunted their red breasts, resting in the old apple tree. Freshly-washed clothes hung from the clothes line, the aroma of home-made

The Secret

bread filled the air. Matthew was playing tag with his friends, their voices occasionally intruding upon the silence of the day. Nan rocked in her favourite chair, knitting a pair of socks for Matthew. Pap rested on a cot enjoying a mid-afternoon smoke. The world is calm and everyone is at peace.

A faint putt-putt comes from down the bay. Soon an unfamiliar white motor boat is anchored in front of our house. On its bow, in black letters, *The Optimist*.

A dory is dropped from its side. A handsome young man with golden blond hair helps a lady into the dory. They row in my direction. I race towards the beach and then stop dead in my tracks. A beautiful lady with soft, brown hair and arching eyebrows stands before me. She looks familiar – something about her reminds me of Nan.

I watch her movements. I admire her navy knee-length uniform, her black oxford shoes and navy-and-white hat. When I grow up I want to look important, just like her.

She races to me and takes me in her arms. "My dear baby girl, how much I have missed you," she says. "Look how much you have grown."

"Mother?"

"Yes darling."

"Let's hurry – we must get Nan and Pap," I say.

I can't take my eyes off my mother's white-gloved hand holding mine. We walk towards the house.

"Hello, Mother," says Elizabeth.

Pap bolts to Nan's side. His face turns white. "Elizabeth, is dat you?"

Mother rushes into Pap's arms. "Patrick and I are home for good," she says.

"Dear Lord, I'm not seeing a spirit – it is you, Elizabeth." Nan says.

"Yes," says Elizabeth. "And Patrick will be here as soon as he gets the boat tied up."

Matthew runs in to the house, straight to Elizabeth's arms. "Sis, where have you been?"

Elizabeth ruffles his hair. "Oh Matthew, you look so handsome. I've missed you so."

Then all eyes turn to the tall, handsome man in the doorway. My father reaches for me. We touch. The house is full of laughter and tears. Our family is whole.

CHAPTER 17

Andrew's Cove

"Pap, will you tell me how Andrew's Cove got its name?" I said. It was the first week of September and the whole family was going on our annual berry-picking trip. Word had it, Andrew Coven hadn't let us down. There were supposed to be more blueberries and partridge berries in the hills surrounding the cove than the whole village could ever use.

"First," said Pap, "we got to load me boat."

Every berry season since I could remember, Pap made a point of telling Matthew and me the legend. It started when Pap was a boy. His grandfather, whom he called Bubba, spared no details about the life and times of Andrew Coven. Since then, the story had became a Dearing tradition.

Each time Pap told it he began with Andrew's mother, Mrs. Coven. People claimed she had special powers. She could make warts disappear by spitting on them, and calm stormy waters with the wave of her hand. It was amazing enough that her chickens laid all winter long. But when her eggs, without the help of a rooster, produced perfect chicks, people labelled Mrs. Coven a witch.

Bubba swore Mrs. Coven knew immediately when someone passed on, or when a child was born and could predict whether it was a boy or a girl. Most people feared her and at night, wouldn't be caught dead passing alone in front of her house. It didn't help she only ever wore black. Bubba, on the other hand, said she was the kindest woman he had ever known. She made the best partridge berry jam he ever tasted and her blueberry tarts simply melted in his mouth.

"Rose, sit on da back thwart," Pap said. "Matthew, take da middle seat. And, Patience, you take the seat at da very front." We climbed aboard and Pap pushed the long white river boat away from the beach. The outboard motor roared a moment later.

On the day Andrew was born, Andrew's father was found dead in his woodhouse, face blown completely off. Some claimed he shot himself. Bubba said it was an accident. Poor Mrs. Coven, what was she to do? Celebrate the birth of her son? Or mourn the death of her husband?

At the age of four, Andrew set fire to the henhouse, burnt the chickens to a crisp. At seven he started a fire in the school. At twelve, he tied two cats together, doused them in kerosene oil and lit them. Mrs. Coven spent many a sleepless night, scared to death her house would go up in flames.

Matthew deflected the spray from the boat with his hand at my face. We splashed each other until Nan made us stop. After awhile I started thinking about Andrew again.

Andrew took to stealing money from the church collection plate, wash from the clotheslines, wood from the neighbours. He lied to his mother, the neighbours, even the parson. And as the days went by he got lazier. Finally Mrs. Coven, suffering from the strain of Andrew's behaviour, found it hard to cope. Her trips to town became fewer and fewer. Then she stopped altogether. Andrew couldn't be depended on to look after Mrs. Coven in the best of conditions. After her cataracts left her nearly blind, Bubba and a few of his cousins took over, making sure she got wood, water and a meal each day.

One year Andrew took his boat and headed down the bay, into open waters, looking for new berry grounds. Berry picking was one thing that interested him.

"Almost there," Pap shouted. Seagulls screeched above our heads. A squirt of bird poop splattered Nan's glasses. The beach was dotted with tents. Everyone came to Andrew's Cove for berries.

The night after Andrew took off in his boat, the smell of smoke woke up Dearing Bay. Down where Andrew had gone, miles and miles of raging orange flames danced.

The next day Mrs. Coven hobbled into the village, the first time in many years. Children clung to their mothers' skirts. People stopped talking. Every eye was on the blind woman leaning on her cane. Mrs. Coven said she had had a premonition. Andrew has become one with the orange flames he was always attracted to. He went in search of berries. Now there would be berries for everyone at Andrew's Cove. *My son's death shall bear fruit.*

There were torrential rains that night and the next morning Bubba found Mrs. Coven. She had died with a smile on her face.

"Mrs. Coven's last words are as true as the Bible," said Pap. The bushes near our tent were laden with ripe, plump blueberries. Pap popped a handful in his mouth. "Andrew might had been as lazy as a cut dog when he was alive, but he sure paid up fer it since hes death."

"Perhaps this time we'll see Andrew's spirit," I said.

"Good chance," said Pap, eyes twinkling. "Let's go pick some berries."

I stepped from bank to bank of the path trying not to get my feet wet. The muddy woodroad didn't slow Matthew down. He'd worn his knee-high rubber boots.

"I told you to wear yours," said Matthew, "but you wouldn't listen to me. I hope you get your feet soaking wet."

"Nan, Matthew is tormenting me."

'You two stop it now or I will take you both back to da tent," Nan said.

I finally caught up with Matthew. He pointed to my mud-caked shoes and soaking feet. He smirked but knew better than say a single word. Neither of us wanted to miss out on filling our stomachs. "Let's run ahead and find a good spot," he said.

There were berries for everyone just like Mrs. Coven had promised. We picked and picked until the sun was about to set. Between the four of us we had two five-gallon buckets filled to their brims.

Just before we got to the wet spot, Matthew, racing ahead of me again, tripped and tore a hole in the foot of his rubber boot. I laughed. "I wonder whose feet will be wet now," I said.

Andrew's Cove

Matthew got mad and pushed me. I held onto him. We both fell in the mud. We could hear Nan and Pap coming.

"We are dead, Matthew."

Pap put his heavy buckets down and glared at us. "If I had any sense, I would put da two of you in me boat and take you home right now," he said.

"Git ahead of me," said Nan. "Der is no peace taking da two of yous anywhere."

Matthew and I marched ahead, scraping the mud off our clothes with our fingernails. We didn't say a word all the way back.

"Now, take dem filthy clothes off," Nan said. "Git every speck cleaned off. Or, nar bite of supper, will either of you get." I doubted she would follow through on her threat but we took no chances. Matthew and I scrubbed our clothes in salt water off the rocks where Pap's boat was moored. The soap would not lather but we didn't complain. Neither of us could bear the thought of being banished to our tent and missing out on the campfire.

We helped Nan prepare supper and minded our manners, especially when other berry pickers stopped for a chat. After supper Matthew made tea and served it to Nan and Pap who were down by the water edge watching the sun set. I cleaned the dishes.

Later, one by one, people lit their camp fires. Little orange balls of flame dotted the shoreline for miles. Would Pap light ours? Would Nan let him?

Pap stood up and stretched. Nan picked up their tea cups. "Rose, did you bring any new potatoes?" said

Pap. "Dey would be some good roasted over a open fire with a bit of salt fish."

Soon our campfire was as big and bright as the others on the beach. Pap told us a tale about his days living with the Micmac Indians on the Goose River. Nan remembered her uncle, whose spirit still roamed the old woodroad where he was last seen alive. Matthew and I listened, munching on roasted spuds and salt caplin. Andrew Coven slipped in and out of my mind, even after everyone had gone back to the tent.

I was staring at our dying fire when I felt a presence around me – something good but unexplainable – like the bond Nan and I had, but never talked about. Perhaps Andrew and Mrs. Coven had found each other at Andrew's Cove. Perhaps they were watching me now. Maybe that was the reason this place brought joy to all who came.

Nan called me for bed. "Another busy day tomorrow."

I took one last look along the beach at the hazy bonfires. Suddenly a cold mist engulfed me. My hair stood on the back of my neck. Goose bumps covered my flesh. A foghorn blared out at sea and I dove into the tent.

"You look like you jest seened Andrew's spirit," Pap said.

CHAPTER 18

Jake the Snake

I RAN TO MEET DAVID, my book bag bouncing against my thigh. Normally, in September I looked forward to school. I loved the books, the new ideas, the learning and I especially loved being with my friends. This fall I had mixed feelings. Mr. Jake was going to be our teacher again.

David, black circles under his eyes, walked slowly with his shoulders hunched over. He had good reason to dread going to school today.

"I didn't tell Grandpa Edwards about the strappings," he said. "But I'm going to tell if Mr. Jake touches me this year." Last year Mr. Jake had strapped David for not understanding a problem in math. Another time, he got it for questioning a theory in science. David and the rest of us kept silent about what went on in school. Mr. Jake promised he would deal severely with tattle-tales.

"Sooner or later he'll get his dues," I said.

The bell rang. We walked to our desks with no rushing or pushing. There were twenty-two of us, grades one to ten. "Turn to the first full page of review in your math books and do all of the sums," said Mr. Jake. "Grades three and down – print your ABCs." Mr. Jake sat down, put his legs up on his desk and read a pocket novel. We were ignored till lunch. This was going to be a very trying year.

"I hate Mr. Jake," I said when I got home. "He is a rotten teacher. I wish he'd get fired."

"Patience, you shouldn't be talking about Mr. Jake like dat," said Nan. "Seems to be a nice enough man – fills in for da parson some Sundays. Does a good job on his sermons."

"Shut up, Patience," said Matthew. If it got out I was a tattle-tale, we'd both get it tomorrow.

"I won't shut up," I said. It was time people knew the real Mr. Jake and I didn't leave out any details. "David isn't the only one who has been punished for no good reason. He strapped Matthew too."

"Is dat right son?" Pap asked.

"Yes sir," said Matthew.

Nan looked shocked. "Why would he strap you, son?"

Matthew glanced at me. "Well, it had to do with Patience," he said. "He made her stand in the corner, holding a stack of books above her head. Her arms got tired. A book fell down and she started crying. Mr. Jake hit her across the back with the strap. He went to hit her again, but –"

"Matthew jumped in between the strap and me," I said. "That made Mr. Jake very angry."

"I see," said Pap.

Nan was speechless. Pap rubbed his chin. He only did that when he was upset. "I think you should tell Rose and me stuff like dat in da future," he said. Nan nodded. For once words had failed her.

A few weeks later, Mr. Edwards, face bright red, came to see Pap. David must have told him about the strapping he'd gotten that day. I'd already told Nan and Pap. I overheard Mr. Edwards say, "Dis better be da last time anything like dis happens or we'll strap his –" Mr. Edwards stopped talking when he saw me. Pap sent me outside then, and I didn't get to hear anymore even though I hovered as close to the house as I dared.

In late November a flu bug hit Dearing Bay that affected the adults more than the children. Nan and Pap were sick in bed. I cooked them hot cereal and tidied the kitchen. While I dumped the slop pail, full of vomit and diarrhoea, in the outhouse, Matthew brought in the wood and water. It was their third day down with the flu. I couldn't remember the last time either of my grandparents had been this sick.

"We're going to be late for school," Matthew said.

Our hearts sank when we reached the school house. Everyone was inside. We quietly walked in, heading for our seats. The clock read two minutes after nine.

"Don't bother sitting down," Mr. Jake said. "Get your hides up here. And hold out your hands."

Matthew and I walked slowly to the front of the classroom. I noticed David biting his bottom lip, no doubt, the sting of the strap fresh in his mind.

Mr. Jake took out his big leather strap. "Hold them out and don't pull back," he said. Four shaking hands pushed out toward him.

Mr. Jake appeared to enjoy himself more with each smack of the strap. Matthew bit into his lower lip trying hard not to cry. I did the same.

This infuriated Mr. Jake. He hit us until our hands and wrists were a brilliant red. Then he ordered us back to our seats.

Matthew and I headed for the door. David, leaving his books behind, followed. "Where are you going?" Mr. Jake yelled. "David, you sit down now! You can't walk out of here. I am your teacher. Obey me this second."

Mr. Jake came after David, landing a blow across his back with the strap. David stumbled.

"You're not a teacher," I cried. You're – you're a monster."

The three of us ran all the way home. Pap looked like death warmed over. Nan's face, burning with fever, was as red as our hands. Pap dragged himself out of bed, staggered, caught himself on the dresser. Trembling, he pulled on his clothes, not bothering to wash up or shave. By then, Mr. Edwards was already pacing our kitchen.

David had Prince hitched up. Mr. Edwards grabbed the reins. Pap climbed on, coughing and sneezing and holding his stomach. Matthew, David and I jumped on just as Mr. Edwards commanded the horse to go.

Pap and Mr. Edwards barged in on Mr. Jake. Mr. Edwards shook his fist in Mr. Jake's face. Pap picked up the strap.

"Children, go outside," said Mr. Edwards.

At first we couldn't hear anything. Then there was yelling. It sounded like Mr. Jake. Finally the door opened and Mr. Jake stumbled out, face flushed. He struggled with his suspenders.

"Oh my God," said one of the grade ten boys. "Jake the Snake got his ass tanned."

CHAPTER 19

Learning Goes Beyond the Classroom

"WE HAVE A NEW TEACHER," said David. He had ran all the way to our house to tell Matthew and me the news. We hadn't had school for a month. It wasn't easy to find a replacement for Mr. Jake. "Grandpa says he's very young – not more than nineteen or twenty. This'll be his first teaching job."

"When will he be here?" I couldn't wait for school to start again.

"Monday morning," said David. He looked at Matthew, eyes wide. "There's more! He loves to play baseball and hockey."

"Now that'll be a welcome change from Jake the Snake," said Matthew

"I dare say only boys will be allowed to play," I said. Why couldn't I have been born a boy? I loved doing all of the so called boy things – sports, target shooting, fishing, tree climbing, and cowboys and robbers. I hated pretty dresses and tea parties. Pretending to be a mother to a doll was not my idea of a good time.

David placed his hand on my shoulder. "Patience, Mr. Waterman will have to take you. You're the best catcher we have. Even better than your Uncle Matthew here." He punched Matthew on the shoulder. "And you can bat the ball just as far."

"Well, maybe it wouldn't hurt for Patience to play with her dolls. They are just collecting dust," Matthew said, eyes twinkling just like Pap's.

I pushed Matthew. He relented and put his arm around my neck. "David is right. We can't do without you."

Finally it was Monday morning. David and I were raring to go but Matthew moped all the way. Now that school was starting again he couldn't go moose hunting with Pap. He'd been practising with the twenty-two and could hit a tin can dead on every time. How he'd wanted to say he killed his first moose! He had hoped he'd be excused from school just this once, but Pap would not hear of it.

Mr. Waterman, close to six feet, stood by the door, bell in hand. He looked much younger than I had expected. "Good morning. Good morning," he said as each student passed by. His eyes were kind and gentle, not stone-cold like Mr. Jake's.

We took our seats. Mr. Waterman closed the door and went to sit on his desk. All eyes were on him. "I am Bert Waterman... eh, Mr. Waterman," he said. "Let's do a roll call, so I can tell who's who." He walked to the blackboard. "Let's talk a bit about expectations, especially what you expect from me."

I looked across at Matthew. He was staring at Mr. Waterman, moose hunting forgotten. A teacher asking us what our expectations were! What next?

"Perhaps I can get us started," said Mr. Waterman, picking up a piece of chalk. "A fair expectation would

Learning Goes Beyond the Classroom

be that I help you when you don't understand something."

Heads nodded in agreement.

Mr. Waterman wrote it on the board. "Another expectation might be that I will treat you equally and fairly."

Again, heads nodding. A few voices, barely audible, managed a *yes*.

"Now, I need to hear from you," said Mr. Waterman.

David bravely spoke up. "I expect that you won't strap me for having a different opinion or if I don't understand something."

"I expect that you will acknowledge me when I raise my hand," said Matthew.

"I expect that you will do your best to help us learn," said Hilda Mae.

"I expect that you will let girls play sports," I said, heart in my throat. I could feel my face getting hot. "If girls want to, that is."

"I agree with you," said Mr. Waterman. "What is your name again?"

"Patience, sir. Patience Dearing."

Mr. Waterman wrote my words on the blackboard. I knew I was going to like our new teacher from that moment on. Later, I noted *Students' Expectations* in my secret notebook on teachers, just below the words *Don't treat people like Mr. Jake*.

It didn't take Mr. Waterman long to get to know the people of Dearing Bay. He visited the homes of his students and didn't mind giving a helping hand at chopping wood or shovelling snow. Being a bachelor, his only charge was a meal once in a while. He often stayed for supper at our house. Nan never saw it as extra work. Matthew and I certainly didn't mind. Having company meant Nan would serve special cakes and cookies she kept hidden for unexpected guests.

"Stay fer a bite to eat," Nan said, one evening after Mr. Waterman had just given Pap a hand in the barn.

"That would be lovely Mrs. Dearing," he said, eying the steaming meat and vegetables on the table.

"Take hold, Mr. Waterman," said Nan. "There is plenty to go around."

Later Nan passed around a plate filled with rich molasses cake. "Mrs. Dearing," said Mr. Waterman, "tis better than what me own mother made when she was alive, God rest her soul."

"Yur poor mother would turn o'er in her grave, if she heard you say such things," scolded Nan. But she looked pleased and quickly poured him another cup of tea.

"Rose can make some good cake – better den me own mother's," said Pap, licking the icing from his teeth.

"Oh Tom," said Nan, blushing at our laughter.

"I wonder why Mr. Waterman spends so much time here," I said later when Matthew and I were doing our homework. Mr. Waterman had gone back outside with Pap to finish up in the barn.

"I have a sneaking feeling that he has a crush on Jessica," said Matthew.

I stopped adding up numbers. Jessica Sheppard lived next door and she was engaged to the minister's son. "Matthew, we have to find out for sure."

"It's none of our business."

I yanked his workbook. "I heard Mrs. Sheppard tell Nan that Jessica and Max are getting married in the summer!"

The following Sunday Mr. Waterman came to visit again. Shortly after supper, he bid us good night.

Matthew jumped up from the couch, ready to put our plan in action. "The tide is up," he said. "Patience, do you remember if we tied up the boat?"

"Oh my," I said. "We better check."

"Don't you two be long," Pap called after us.

We waited outside and a minute later we heard a whistle. It came from the back of the woodhouse, an area hidden from the road.

"Let's go up on the barn roof," whispered Matthew. We crept up the ladder and crawled to the edge of the roof, thankful for the full moon. Below us Mr. Waterman paced back and forth. Within minutes a woman joined him. They fell into each others arms, and kissed.

"I love you, Jess," Mr. Waterman said.

"I love you too, Bert," Jessica said. They kissed again and again. Matthew and I dared not move. We had never seen anything like this.

Mr. Waterman sat on a pile of lumber stacked against the woodhouse. He reached for Jessica's hand. "Have you told Max about us yet?"

Jessica let him pull her into his lap. "He knows something is wrong. When he calls on me, I make excuses." She stood up. "He's a nice man. I don't want to hurt his feelings. And Mother – well, I don't know what to say to her. She'd already got the church hall booked for a June wedding, for goodness sake."

Mr. Waterman stood up and faced Jessica. "I want you to tell Max and your parents about us," he said. "I'd rather they find out from you than someone else."

Too late, I thought.

"I promise I'll tell Mom and Dad tonight," said Jessica. "I'll give Max back his engagement ring tomorrow."

Mr. Waterman took Jessica's hand again. "I'm glad you're not wearing it tonight," he said. They kissed, held hands and then finally tore themselves apart.

"Good-night, my darling Jessica," Mr. Waterman hoarsely whispered after her.

"Good night, my love," she softly called back.

Matthew and I stayed on top of the barn until we were certain Mr. Waterman had left. He'd be very disappointed in what we'd done. Nan and Pap wouldn't be happy either. But to have witnessed true love firsthand was worth the risk. Matthew and I vowed we'd keep Mr. Waterman's secret safe.

"I was about to comed down to da beach and look fer you," Pap said, meeting us at the door.

"Beach?"

"Yes, da beach," Pap said. "I take it you have tied da boat up fer da night."

※ ※ ※

Learning Goes Beyond the Classroom

Three months later Mr. Waterman and Jessica Sheppard were married. Pap lifted his glass in the air. "A toast to the bride and groom."

"A toast to my best man, Tom Dearing," said Mr. Waterman. "And thank's for feeding me so many nights, Mrs. Dearing." He winked. Pap winked back.

Before Jessica left for her honeymoon, I overheard her thanking Nan for not letting the cat out of the bag. I got the idea that my grandparents knew all along about Mr. Waterman and Jessica.

Six months after their wedding Jessica gave birth to identical twin girls. It was the talk of the village. Matthew and I couldn't understand why adults whispered about the Waterman twins when children were around. It took me a while to solve the mystery.

"Matthew, I read today that it takes nine months for a baby to grow inside its mother's womb," I said. By now the twins were learning to crawl. Mr. and Mrs. Waterman and Nan and Pap were playing cards at the kitchen table while Matthew and I minded the girls in the living room.

"It's not nine months," said Matthew. "Mr. Waterman and Jessica were married only six months when the babies were born, so it has to be six months."

"But the book said nine months. I'll show you." I got the book from its hiding spot in my bedroom. It was Nan's book and had lots of interesting reading about private parts of the human body, even pictures of grown men and women.

"Well, the book is wrong, Patience. I'm going to ask Mr. Waterman. He'll tell you the book is wrong," said Matthew. "Mr. Waterman! Mr. Waterman!"

"What is it, Matthew?"

"Patience's book says a baby takes nine months to grow in its mother's body. It must be wrong because you were married only six months when the twins were born."

Jessica turned white. Nan, eyes boring at me, grabbed her apron. Pap took his pipe out of his mouth. Mr. Waterman's Adam's apple bobbed up and down. "Tell her, Mr. Waterman, that the book is wrong."

"Patience Dearing," said Nan, grabbing the book out of my hands. "How dare you take dis from me room."

"If you don't mind, Rose and Tom, I'll have a word with Matthew and Patience," said Mr. Waterman. "I did promise them on my first day of school that I would help when they didn't understand something. It seems to me they could do with my help right about now." He reached for his coat. "Come on, Matthew and Patience, let's go for a walk down on the beach."

Still clutching the book, Nan glanced at Pap for support, then turned to Mr. Waterman. "Dey is children, you know, so dey don't need to know everything about da grown-up ways," she said.

Too late, I thought, but I wasn't about to tell Nan I'd already read all the parts about babies and how they were made. And I'd never forget the colour pictures of how it was done.

"Don't you worry, Mrs. Dearing. There's lots of things to learn," said Mr. Waterman. "This is a good example of where learning goes beyond the classroom."

CHAPTER 20

Troubled Times

"Patience, looks like we can haul our wood out today," said David. Every Saturday since early winter, David and I had strapped on our snowshoes and headed for the woods with axes in hand, determined to cut and deliver our share of firewood.

"Yeah," I said, trying to sound excited. I couldn't get my mind off Matthew. Lately, he didn't want anything to do with me. All he cared about was spending time with his older friends. Yesterday, I smelled smoke on his breath. It seemed to me Matthew was up to no good.

"I was just thinking about our first day in the woods," said David. "Remember how long it took us to chop down our very first tree?"

"It was bloody hard work, that's for sure," I said. "Chopping it down was only half the job. The limbing and stacking nearly killed me." I held up my bare hands. "See these calluses. I thought the blisters would never heal."

"Jump on the sleigh, Patience," said David. "I'll give you a ride." The snow conditions were icy and fast. We would have no trouble hauling all one hundred pieces of wood today – fifty for the Dearings and fifty for the Edwards. "Let's get finished before lunch,

Patience, I can't wait to have some of your Nan's soup."

"I can't wait for your Nan's extra special treat," I said.

Nan and Pap were working in the woodhouse. David was having his second bowl of rabbit soup when Matthew came in with his three new friends. The Harper brothers had recently moved to Dearing Bay from Fogo Island, after their mother was committed to a mental institution in St. John's. Old man Harper claimed to be the only living relative of Andrew and Mrs. Coven and had taken over their rundown property.

"See all our wood, Matthew?" said David.

Matthew grabbed a bun off the table. His eyes were bloodshot again. Like his friends.

"What's that smell?" I said.

Matthew gave me his keep quiet look. The Harper boys stood by the door with brassy grins on their faces. David continued to slurp his soup like nothing new was going on.

"Let's go outside," Matthew said to his friends.

"Can I have your share of the soup?" said David.

"Sure." Matthew closed the door behind him, not looking back.

I was certain Matthew had been drinking. Smoking and drinking. What next? Skipping school, like the Harper boys?

"Let's go to my house now, Patience," said David. "I can't wait to see what Nan's extra special treat is."

"Okay," I said, glad to be getting my mind off Matthew. I loved going to David's house.

Like always, Mrs. Edwards welcomed me with open arms. "Come in, me darlings," she said. "What a fine lot of wood you brought me. Well, goodness sakes, the two of yous is something else. Well. Well. Well." She dug deep into her apron pocket and came up with a dime each. "Enough for a candy bar, I think."

"Thank you very much." I had been eying for a week the new brand of candy bar at the store. They cost fifteen cents. I already had a nickel saved.

"Git out of your snowsuits and come on inside," said Mrs. Edwards. "I have a bit of a grown-up treat fer you today."

In the warm kitchen we watched her take down three fancy long-stemmed wine glasses from the cupboard. "I made some wine out of the blueberries the two of you picked last summer." She brought out a gallon jar from her pantry. "I don't think it will hurt none, if you were to have a little taste." She poured about a half-inch in each glass. "Christmas is just around the corner. So, let's toast. Merry Christmas and may God keep us healthy fer another year."

The taste was sweet and warmed my stomach from the inside out. Other than Holy Communion, I had never had wine before. I wasn't sure if it was drinking the wine itself or drinking wine from a proper wine glass that made me feel grown-up. Whichever, it was different and a little exciting. Was this how Matthew felt?

"Now I'm ready for my grown-up treat," said David.

Mrs. Edwards laughed. "You've had it already."

"Huh," said David. "I have?"

"Yes, you have," said Mrs. Edwards. "Wine is a grown-up treat, to be consumed only at special occasions."

I wondered what special occasion Matthew had been celebrating.

One night a few weeks later Nan and Pap dropped in on the Edwards, leaving Matthew and me alone in the house. My mind was made up. Tonight I was going to talk to him.

"You're going to be in big trouble," I said, cutting myself a huge piece of Christmas cake, "when Nan and Pap can prove what you've been up to."

Matthew put down his raspberry juice. "What are you talking about?"

"Drinking and smoking." I leaned across the table towards him. "These Harper boys, they're up to no good. Don't know why you're so friendly with them."

"Mind your own business," said Matthew, clasping the table edge with both hands.

"I'm telling you for your own good, Matthew," I said. "I think Nan and Pap got some idea what you're doing. Heard them whispering the other night about the Harper boys. Said something about catching them red-handed."

Matthew slumped in his chair. "You did?" For a split-second the old Matthew was sitting across from me. Then he went to his bedroom and closed the door. He hadn't even finished his juice.

※ ※ ※

Our Christmas concert was only a week away. We had a new reverend now and his wife, Mrs. Gibbs, a proper lady from London, England, pumped the organ. The whole school was practising "Silent Night".

"We are as ready as we can be to demonstrate our acting ability and singing talents to our fellow citizens in Dearing Bay," said Mrs. Gibbs. "I am really proud of you. You are good enough for Broadway."

That made us laugh. I doubted if we were as good at acting as Mrs. Gibbs claimed. But I was in no position to second guess the judgement and experience of a well-travelled lady from overseas, who had been to Broadway a time or two.

"A few things to work on over the next few days," she continued. "Hilda Mae, you need to remember your lines just a wee bit better. David, try not to ad lib. And Matthew, for a latecomer, I am really impressed."

I was pleased too. These days Matthew worked hard on everything. The Harper brothers got caught stealing wine from Hilda Mae's parents, and old man Harper let them be sent off to reform school in St. John's. That had really shook up Matthew and, since then, he'd been trying to make amends with Nan and Pap. And with me.

Even though he'd given up the drinking he hadn't gone back to being the old Matthew. I knew he still had a smoke off and on. He'd grown up in the last month and things like the Christmas concert were babyish for him. But he knew how much he had disappointed Nan and Pap and me and that's why he was putting so much effort into the concert.

"Now, Patience," said Mrs. Gibbs. "Your singing..."

"I take after Pap when it comes to singing," I said.

"She likes to carry her own tune," said Matthew.

Mrs. Gibbs laughed. "I've noticed that about you Dearings."

The evening before the concert, Pap and Mr. Edwards brought the Christmas tree, a ceiling-high fir. "Ready to decorate," said Mr. Edwards.

Mrs. Gibbs asked Matthew to attach the final decoration and when the star was in place on top of the tree, we all stepped back to admire our masterpiece.

Tinsel glittered from the reflections of the fire in the stove and the kerosene lamps in each corner of the hall, reminding me of the northern lights. Peace and love filled the room. I tucked my arm in Matthew's. He did not pull away.

"We have electric tree lights back home in London," said Mrs. Gibbs. "But this is just as pretty." I was certain she was thinking of her family far across the Atlantic. When she started to sing "Away in a Manger", I reached for her hand. She looked at me and smiled. My singing was off-key but I didn't care. Everyone else joined in one by one including Mr. Edwards. And Pap. No one paid any attention to Pap and me singing our own way.

On the big night, Mrs. Gibbs took us aside for one last time. "How many of you have butterflies in your stomachs?"

We all put up our hands except Hilda Mae's little brother Henry. Deadly serious, he said, "I didn't eat no butterflies for supper, Mrs. Gibbs."

"It's good to be nervous before a performance. It brings out the best in you," said Mrs. Gibbs. "Remember you are good enough for Broadway." Her words were so sincere and convincing, I honestly believed we could walk on water. "It's time for the show," she said. "Break a leg."

"But," said Henry, "if I break a leg, I won't be able to do my part."

David peeped around the curtain. "The place is packed," he said, and then it was time to take our places on stage for the opening song, "Oh, Canada". For the first time, I didn't sing off-key. Mrs. Gibbs looked up from her organ and winked, as pleased with me as I was with myself.

We went through skit after skit. Matthew played the perfect Santa Claus. I was Mrs. Claus. Hilda Mae played Mrs. Gibbs. The audience cheered at how perfectly she imitated Mrs. Gibbs's English accent. David sang "Jingle Bells" all alone, and he did not ad lib once. Our family and friends laughed at our jokes and applauded our performances.

Then in pure Newfoundland Christmas tradition, we dressed in costumes and masks to keep our identity a secret and came back on stage. "Any mummers in the night?" we cackled and squeaked in fake voices. Mrs. Gibbs, who had no idea what a mummer was just a few short months ago, wore a flour-sack hood and a lumber jacket turned inside out.

How surprised Mrs. Gibbs had been when Pap told her about mummers. "Mummering is as traditional to Newfoundlanders at Christmas as plum pudding is to the British," he said.

"Let me get this straight," said Mrs. Gibbs. "People dress up to hide who they are. Then they go from house to house to visit friends. They have a little drink, play a little music, have a little dance and then they go to the next house. Unannounced?"

"It's not just friends they visit in their merriment Mrs. Gibbs," I said, "A mummer will visit his foes too at Christmas."

We did perform like stars on Broadway. Our last song, "Ode to Newfoundland", got us a standing ovation.

In the midst of the applause, I could hear jingle bells. All heads turned to greet jolly ole Saint Nick.

"Ho, Ho, Ho," he bellowed. "Ho, Ho, Ho"! "Merry Christmas byes and girls. Merry Christmas to yous." He carried a big red sack bulging with presents.

We gave him a traditional welcome with a round of "For He's a Jolly Good Fellow".

Dear ole Santa Claus danced up the aisle to sit in his special chair by the tree. I watched the little children. How they believed this man was the real Santa that just came down from the North Pole. Not so long ago, I believed like them.

Santa presented each child with a bright red apple, some juicy purple grapes or an orange that the merchants had brought in especially for the holiday season. How we appreciated that. Fresh fruit was seldom available, even in summer.

When my name was called I was as excited as the little boys and girls.

"Have you been a good girl dis year, Patience Dearing?" Santa said.

I looked into Pap's gentle blue eye. "I think so, Santa," I said.

"I hear you have been a very good girl dis year," said Santa, and handed me a juicy apple.

"Thanks Pa – Santa," I said. Apples were my all-time favourite.

Santa reached deep into his bag and came up with one last present.

"For me?" said Mrs. Gibbs. "I wasn't expecting a present, Santa."

"Hurry up, Mrs. Gibbs. Santa gotta git to the narth pole yet tonight," he said. He handed her a big red envelope. "Open it up, me dear. Read it out so da people can hear what it says."

"Merry Christmas," read Mrs. Gibbs. "Now turn around." Turning, she saw her sister from London walk through the door. "Evelyn!"

Later, when she and her sister had finally stopped hugging, Mrs. Gibbs said, "This is the best Christmas present I could ever have."

"I knows what you mean, Mrs. Gibbs," said Santa, gazing over his beard at Nan, Matthew and me with eyes filled with love.

CHAPTER 21

The Winds of Change

"Hilda Mae's mom ordered an electric iron from the catalogue," I said, carrying a hot iron from the stove to the kitchen table. I was about to press my shirt. Now that I was in my teens, wrinkles were no longer acceptable. "I wish we could have one, when the electricity comes."

"Me old iron will do us jest fine," said Nan. "And me lamps." Nan wasn't one bit excited about replacing her kerosene oil lamps with wire, switches and light bulbs. And she certainly wasn't interested in electric stoves and television sets.

"David's place is getting wired tomorrow," I said. "Mrs. Edwards likes the idea of having lights in every room." I dropped the old-fashioned iron on the stove to reheat. "I heard her say so myself."

Nan stopped knitting, wool wrapped around her thumb and forefinger. "Mrs. Edwards changed her mind?"

"Only after Mr. Jackson told her about the comforts of electricity," I said. "He said he'd show Mr. Edwards how to wire his place. It would be cheap to do." The Jacksons were the only people in the village who had electricity and all of its modern conveniences. They'd been fortunate enough to own a diesel generator for the last few years. "Mr. Jackson says he can't wait for the main power supply. Won't have to worry about running out of fuel or generator breakdowns any more."

Nan resumed knitting. "Everything's changing around me. You is changing too, Patience. Here you is all dressed up. Ready for James Jackson to come by." She sighed. "Only like yesterday, you spent all your time under me watchful eye. You and Matthew. Or you and David, down on the beach."

David and I used to spend hours catching minnows for Nan's ducks and digging clams for Mrs. Edwards and Nan's chickens. Clam pissing was our funniest game. Look how far mine pissed, I'd say when a clam squirted my face. Mine pissed just as far, David would retort. Sometimes, trying to get the clams to spurt further our fingers broke through the shells into the flesh. Hungry seagulls gobbled up the exposed meat.

One time when David and I were out in Grandfather's old black dory looking at the ever-changing ocean bottom, I tried to tell David that things were changing for me too. I blamed it on Mother Nature. A month later he came by after a rainstorm, wanting me to ride bikes with him through the water-filled potholes. I had just fixed my hair and applied a little light powder to my cheeks. My girlfriends and I were going up the road and I was hoping to see James Jackson.

David's head dropped. I knew how he felt. A few years ago, I had felt the same when Matthew no longer wanted to do things with me. I asked David if he remembered our talk in the dory.

"Well, Mother Nature is doing her changes on me now," I said. "Nan calls it growing up. It happened to

Matthew and now it's my turn." Facing him, I rested both hands on his shoulders. "It will happen to you too."

"Can we still be friends, Patience?"

"I will always be your friend, David."

Later I watched him and some younger children zooming through the potholes on their bikes. Their laughter echoed into my bedroom. In a way I missed not being with them. On the other hand, the uncertainty ahead was strangely more appealing.

"James is here," said Nan, interrupting my thoughts.

James Jackson, a well-mannered boy, could pick any girl he wanted. His family was considered rich by our standards and James always had the newest and best of everything. It was a real treat to be invited to his house to watch television, even if the diesel ran out now and then.

"Mrs. Dearing, when are you going to get your house wired?" said James. "The power will be here in a week or two."

"I dare say, I'll be one of the last," said Nan, needles picking up speed. "Things is changing too darn fast fer me liking."

The night the power switch was scheduled to be turned on, Matthew, James and I were ice skating on a little pond not too far from our house. The sky above was filled with millions of twinkling stars. The big full moon seemed close enough to touch. Frost glistened on the ground. The bright northern lights danced along the edges of the wondrous dome above our heads.

Suddenly orangy-yellow electrical lights flooded the night in all directions. Up and down the bay, as far as we could see, more and more lights brightened our isolated world as every single electrical switch in Dearing Bay was turned on.

For a moment not one of us could move or say a word. Then our eyes circled right around the bay. We gawked at all the lights. It was pretty. It was awesome. It was modern!

"Wow!" I yelled. "Dearing Bay has arrived."

"Connection to the outside world," shouted Matthew.

"No more diesel fuel for the generator," screamed James.

"Look how bright it is!" I said. "I can see so much farther." I skated to the other end of the pond, Matthew and James close behind.

"I wonder how many lights there are," said James.

"Let's count them," said Matthew. We each came up with a different number, each insisting we were right.

"Let's count the stars instead," said James, lying on his back, pointing towards the sky.

"There seems to be fewer," I said. "And the northern lights are dimmer." Had the bright beauty of the heavens taken cover from the artificial lights that now replaced it?

Some of the spirit left me. I no longer felt like skating. I realized that for everything gained in the name of progress, something surely would be lost, often something precious that could never be replaced.

I pulled on my brown snow boots and slowly headed home, skates slung over my shoulder. There were no bright orangy-yellow lights shining from our windows. Instead, there was the familiar blue-and-yellow glow from the kerosene oil lamp. Pap and Nan

The Winds of Change

were not yet ready for man-made changes. They needed to hang onto the old a bit longer. Tonight, I understood why.

For the first month-and-a-half, every house had every light on from dark to bedtime. The first power bill smartened people up, just like Pap said it would.

But electricity was here to stay. Soon roads were pushed through to other communities and a causeway built across the bay. Indoor plumbing became popular and televisions and electrical appliances standard items in a home. Lifestyles changed too. Cars and trucks. Shopping in town. People stayed home and watched television. Somehow there was no longer time to visit dear friends and relatives.

The Dearing house was the last to throw out its kerosene lamps. Nan had put up a good fight but as I explained to her and Pap, change was both good and bad. Good things were gained and good things were lost. We could try and fight it, but progress, like Mother Nature, would always get the upper hand.

The winds of change were blowing strong across our village.

"Da kitchen is some bright," said Nan when Pap threw on the switch for the first time. Matthew switched the outside lights off and on. I tried the porch. Nan slowly walked into the living room and tried the light there. Then my old-fashioned Grandmother went around and shut off all the lights except the one in the kitchen.

Not everything was changing.

CHAPTER 22

High School

OUTSIDE OUR HOME, though, change was everywhere. Our one-room Anglican Church school became the latest victim, replaced by a brand new all-denominational high school.

The day after Labour Day, a big yellow school bus turned the corner to take us into this new world called high school. Not one of us had seen a bus before. Now we were actually going to ride on one.

"Here it comes," someone shouted.

"Let's ride in the back," said a boy.

"I want to ride in the front," said another.

The bus pulled up in front of us. Two doors swung open. So that was how we got inside the big yellow container. All of us rushed at the same time. Someone fell. The rest of us landed on top, with arms, legs, lunchboxes and books all in a heap in front of the open doors.

The bus driver rocked back and forth with laughter. "I sure hope yous feel dis eager comed June."

I picked myself up, straightened my clothes and walked on the empty bus like a little lady. I choose a seat in the middle, giving no consideration to the front or the back. James sat beside me. The others picked seats as close to us as they could.

High School

I studied the dark green interior, noticed the windows opened and caught the driver's eyes looking at us in the mirror. David was sitting close to Hilda Mae and holding her hand. Mother Nature had finally caught up with him, too.

We picked up strangers along the way. They were all orderly, not like us. They didn't talk much. Did they know exactly what to do or were they half-scared to death too?

After forty minutes on dusty roads, we pulled into the school parking lot. Five other buses pulled up, one after the other. I had never seen so many people in my life. There were more here than in my entire village. And the school. It was huge, as big as twenty or more village homes joined together.

My first trip up the corridor to my homeroom I barely took in the freshly painted walls and polished tile floors. Mostly, I noticed the other students. God, I was the youngest person here.

"Are you lost, little girl?" said a tall boy. He looked eighteen.

"No," I said.

"This is grade ten," he said.

"Yes, it is," I said, thankful when our homeroom teacher walked in and introduced herself. She was from Ottawa. I couldn't help notice how odd she sounded with her careful pronunciation of every word. No slang. Not one *dat* or *dem*.

I wished I could see James Jackson's face, but he was sitting in front of me. I glanced over at Hilda Mae, the only other person I knew. For once, I was glad she was in my class.

"Patience Dearing," said Mrs. Hydro. "My records say that you are fourteen. Is that correct?"

"Yes, Ma'am," I said.

"And, you are in the correct class?"

"Yes, Ma'am," I said, sitting up as straight as I could. "Grade ten."

"You are very young for grade ten, dear."

"I'll be *fifteen* before da school year ends."

I could tell Mrs. Hydro thought I was too young for grade ten but she finished roll call and sent us off to the gym.

Never, in my wildest dreams, had I envisaged a room this big and high. The gym even had a cafeteria. Children poured in through the four separate doors, quickly filling up the rows of seats.

A blond middle-aged man walked on stage, dressed in a black suit and tie. He introduced himself as Mr. Irwin, the principal. He talked about teachers and buzzers and rules and schedules until the words started to leak out of my ears. I'd never keep it all straight. Did everyone from Toronto like to hear himself talk? Mr. Irwin mentioned something about school monitors, whatever that was, and we were dismissed.

"Well, dat was short and to da point."

I turned to look at the boy sitting next to me. He had red hair and freckles, and he flashed me a cheeky grin. "Me name is Fred Farris." I smiled back, relieved at least one stranger at my new school sounded like me.

"So, Patience Dearing," Fred said, when we were settled in our first classroom. "Is you really dat smart?"

"I guess."

He looked me over. "Cocky too, eh."

I ignored James' scowl and said, "Bet yur boots, I am."

Fred laughed. "Oh, Patience Dearing, I think I's going to like you."

A few people were brave enough to make the rounds and introduce themselves, but we mostly huddled with children from our own villages, waiting for a teacher to show up. There were twenty-three of us. Fifteen boys and eight girls, everyone older and taller than me.

Suddenly Fred tipped the garbage can over and stepped up on it. "Who wants to get kicked out?"

Half a dozen hands shot up, mostly older boys.

"Who wants to do nothing?"

No hands. We were all wondering what Fred was up to.

Fred jumped off the garbage can. "Who wants to do something?"

Half the class responded.

"Seems to me, we have voted for something," Fred said, looking completely at home sitting behind the teacher's desk. "What do you want to do?"

"Tease the girls."

"Write a dirty joke on the blackboard for Mrs. Hydro."

"Throw paper kites at all the girls we want to date this year."

After the boys ran out of ideas a homely girl suggested we do school work and was immediately shouted down.

"We could take turns," I said. "Talk about where we're from, what we did this summer…"

My voice died away, and I sat down quickly.

"Don't all stand up at da same time," Fred said.

That broke the ice. We all laughed. Still, no one wanted to go first.

Fred got up from the teacher's chair and sat on her desk. "I'll go first den. I'm warning you dat once I get started, it might be hard for me to shut me mouth."

"We'll let you know when we've heard enough," James said, just loud enough for me to hear.

"Girls love me," Fred said, and he was off on a long tale about being raised by a grandmother who swore no more of her men were going to drown at sea. "Me grandmother wants me to be a teacher, a doctor, a lawyer or anything," he said, walking back to his own desk, "but she don't want me to be a fisherman like me poor dad."

Ruth Gower from Cow Pond Cove went next. "Population three hundred including every man, woman, child, dog and cow."

One after another, students stood up, some not saying more than a few words, others long-winded. Most of us were the first from our villages to attend high school. The majority of us came from fishing families and knew the agony of disasters at sea. The girls all wanted more than the women they knew had. They wanted a career in teaching, nursing or office work. The boys seemed to have fishing in their blood, but their families all hoped they'd get a profession, or at least a good job that took them far away from the sea. All of our dialects were different. How would Mrs. Hydro understand us?

High School

A tall, handsome boy who had caught the eye of a number of girls, had a different story. His name was Michael Sutherland and his family had recently moved from Halifax. His father was the new Pentecostal minister at Bay St. John.

"Frankly," Michael said, "I don't think I'm going to like living here very much. I'm stuck for the next few years though, until my father gets a new posting. There's nothing to do here and I can't wait to get back to Halifax."

Michael didn't seem to like us much. He didn't even sound like us. But he was from the *city*. Ruth's jaw had dropped as soon as he mentioned Halifax.

"Patience Dearing," Fred said, after everyone had taken their turn. "You is on last."

I felt my blood rush to my face when I stood up. My knees were knocking. Butterflies flew wild in my stomach. I opened my mouth but no words came out. Twenty-two faces looked at me.

"Patience Dearing," said Fred. "I still is curious how you got to be in grade ten. Tell us how come you's so smart."

"I started school when I was four," I said, thankful for Fred's suggestion.

"That's only part of it," said Hilda Mae. "Her Pap threatened the minister. Said he and the whole Dearing family would stop paying the church if Patience couldn't attend school." Hilda Mae stuck her nose in the air, happy to have shared my past with our new classmates.

"That's just rumour, Hilda Mae," said James Jackson. "Patience could read every word in the grade-one books when she was only three, thanks to her Nan. She was ready for school."

My classmates looked from Hilda Mae to James then back to me. "Now you know why I'm in grade ten," I said. "Take your pick as to which story you believe."

Soon, in spite of my age, I fitted in with my classmates. Fred and James competed for my attention and Hilda Mae and I continued to get under each other's skin. I got used to Mr. Irwin's never-ending speeches and my concern about Mrs. Hydro understanding us was needless. She caught on very quickly. Some of her proper English wore off on us but more of our sayings and slang found their way into her grammar.

"Dats da way tis, bye," Mrs. Hydro said one day, explaining something to Fred. *"Now dats done, hand me books o'er will ya, please."*

I watched Mrs. Hydro change the calendar from May to June. I reflected upon the last eight months and how my anxiety had turned to contentment, how strangers slowly changed to friends, and how much high school had opened up my little world of Dearing Bay.

CHAPTER 23

Matthew's Graduation

MATTHEW WAS OFTEN the topic of discussion in the girls' washroom. He was over six feet now, with broad shoulders and slim hips. He looked older than his eighteen years and could easily pass for twenty-one. I couldn't understand why the girls got so excited. Matthew was okay, but lots of boys were far better looking. It was beyond me why girls spent so much time flirting with him, trying to get him to notice them.

"Patience, I'll owe you big time if you can get Matthew to invite me to the graduation dance," said a girl from one of Matthew's classes.

"I'll be your friend for life, if you can get him to ask me," said another. "To be kissed by those lips!" she moaned, puckering her own red lips in the mirror.

Fact was, Matthew hadn't dated any girls in school, despite their huge crushes. As far as I could tell he was interested in nothing but their friendship.

"Matthew was always a bit of mystery to me," said Ruth Gower. "I sense his mind is elsewhere, but I just can't put my finger on it." Ruth liked Matthew but she still had her eye on Michael Sutherland. "But if he wants a date, I'll go with him," she said. "I hear Danielle LeRoche invited Michael and that just burns me up."

Matthew's Graduation

"There are better fish in the ocean than Michael Sutherland," I said.

Then Danielle walked in.

"I'm working on Patience to get Matthew to invite me to the dance," said the girl from Matthew's class.

"Maybe Matthew Dearing doesn't like girls," said Danielle. "He's probably queer. Lots of queers in Montreal, where I came from." She brushed mascara on her already darkened lashes. "A doctor who worked with my dad was queer. He was built like a brick shithouse and just as good-looking as Matthew."

We all stared at Danielle LeRoche in disbelief. Since arriving just after Christmas she had brought a whole new perspective to Spectrum High. Some of her stories where far-fetched, as far as I was concerned, but she swore they were true. "Live in the big city and see for yourself," she said.

"Matthew has a girlfriend already," I said, defending Matthew's reputation. "That's why he doesn't go out with any of you." The words were out of my mouth before I could stop myself. What had I said? Matthew would surely kill me if he found out. The girlfriend part wasn't exactly true.

"A girlfriend?"

"Who is she?"

"Which class is she in?"

One question after another. The blood raced to my face and pounded in my head. I had gone too far.

"We want a name, Patience."

"I'm sworn to secrecy," I said.

The bell rang. "The webs we create," said Ruth, leaving me alone in the washroom.

The truth was I had a sneaking suspicion that Matthew was head-over-heels in love with Becky Sanders. She was three years Matthew's senior, and a mother of a two-year-old boy, Jason. Becky, a widow now, had married just after her sixteenth birthday. Soon after her son was born, her husband failed to return from a hunting trip. A terrible snow storm had come up. Later they found his gun near Ghost Pond, but not a trace of him.

Becky had no living family, other than a father who lived on the west coast, and was left alone to raise her young son. Like most of the village men, Pap and Matthew helped Becky, from time to time, with some of the manly jobs around her house. Jason liked Matthew right off the bat. He called him *Mew*. Lately Matthew was always finding some reason to be at Becky's house. One thing was certain, his eyes lit up every time her name was mentioned.

I got off the school bus that evening and dragged myself inside. "Looks like you have a lot on your mind," Nan said.

"How can we get Becky Sanders to go to the graduation dance with Matthew?"

"Patience Dearing, are you trying to matchmake?"

"Kind of."

"Nice girl, dat Becky," said Nan, taking the cover off the cooking pot. "I've been watching Matthew around her." She added some carrots to the stew, taking her time. She put the cover back on and absently wiped her hands on her apron. "A dance would do dat girl good."

I crossed my fingers, looking towards the sky. "Let it work, Lord. Please let it work."

Nan popped the question during supper. "Son, have you thought of inviting Becky to yur graduation dance?"

"Becky?" He stopped eating, pretending casualness, but his eyes were bright.

"Well, da two of you been friends fer a long time," said Nan, reaching for a slice of bread. "Jason, he could come on over here with Tom and me."

"Do you think she would go?"

"What woman in her right senses wouldn't want to be seen with a handsome chap like you," I said, punching him in the arm.

"I dare say Becky is dying fer you to ask her, me son," said Pap.

A big smile crossed Matthew's face.

"I was going to stop by Becky's myself, after supper," said Nan. She left the table and came back with a wool cap in her hand. "I made dis fer Jason. Perhaps, Matthew, you could take it over fer me instead." Nan yawned. "Would save me from going out. Feel kind of tired tonight fer some reason."

Clever Nan.

The night of the dance the gym looked so beautiful. Ribbons and bows in pink and blue and white and large balloons hung from the ceiling. Each table was set with white linen, shining silverware and long stem glasses. Boys were in dress suits and girls in long dresses. Proud parents and siblings talked and laughed, knowing they were to leave as soon as the dance started. The graduating students were the stars of the night.

Again, the girls' washroom was the meeting place.

"I don't believe it," said the girl from Matthew's class. "Not one of us dated Matthew Dearing all year."

"I hear he didn't ask anybody to the dance," said her friend, powdering her nose. "Guess he's off with his elusive girlfriend." She smirked at me as she spoke.

"My date is no Matthew Dearing, but he will do for tonight," said Hilda Mae. "Too bad you can't stay for the dance, Patience." But she didn't mean it.

Secretly, I wished I could have gone but I didn't get invited. Besides Nan would never let me go even if I were asked. A fifteen-year-old should never date anyone older than sixteen she'd say. And everyone in Matthew's class was at least seventeen.

"I'm convinced Matthew's queer," said Danielle. "Too bad. Such a waste of a body." She adjusted the spaghetti straps on her sleek, black gown. "I must go back and keep Michael company." The door closed behind her.

"Keep Michael company," snickered Ruth, brushing her thick hair ferociously. "Thank goodness, this is her last night in this school."

"And you and Michael have another year," I said. We giggled over that all the way back to the gym.

Nan and Pap and Jason had already taken their seats. The graduating class and their dates were seated at the head table. Two places were still vacant. Where was Matthew? Did Becky change her mind? It was almost time for the opening ceremony.

Then the last two guests arrived. The sparkling beads and sequins on her teal dress were no match for the girl's blue-green eyes. Her long golden hair glistened. She was radiant and could have been mistaken for a movie star. She held out her hand to the young man at her side. And Matthew, in a navy suit, eyes soft under the lights, proudly led Becky Sanders to her seat.

Goose bumps covered my body. I squeezed Nan's hand. She squeezed mine back. Ruth gave me a thumbs-up.

Danielle laughed, and her voice carried down from the head table. "I'll be damned. Matthew Dearing isn't queer after all."

CHAPTER 24

Off to Toronto

ONE SUNDAY AFTER CHURCH we stayed behind for tea. Speculation of Matthew's future and what was best for him had been the topic of conversation for awhile. In many ways it was a curse to have been the first person in the village to graduate from high school. One neighbour suggested that Matthew should leave home to put his education to use. Another said that he may as well have dropped out of school like some of the others if he was just going to stay around the bay.

"Matthew, my boy, when is you going away to use dat learning?" said Mrs. Adams, the village gossip, for the third time this week.

"When hell freezes over," I said.

"Patience, mind you manners," Nan said.

"A few grown-ups around here could do with minding theirs too," I said, looking directly at Mrs. Adams.

Matthew pretended to be very interested in something outside the window.

"Patience," Pap said. "No more!"

I bit my tongue to keep quiet. I wanted to ask them why their own daughters and sons didn't get off their lazy behinds and go somewhere to work. After all, you didn't need a high school diploma to work in a factory on the mainland.

"Mrs. Adams, I's in no rush to see me boy off," said Nan. "Although, I don't agree with Patience's bad manners, there's some truth in what da girl says." She looked around the room. "It really isn't anyone's business what Matthew does."

A hush fell over the hall. "I see," said Mrs. Adams. I'd never heard her at a loss for words before.

Two weeks later, long after I'd put the incident behind me, Matthew came down to the beach looking for me.

"Over here," I said, standing up besides Pap's boat. "I was just reading the new book I got in the mail today." I held it up so Matthew could see. "It's called *Moving On*. About a girl who is leaving home for the first time."

Matthew skipped a rock across the still waters. "Let's go for a walk along the beach," he said.

We walked along the water edge with our heads down. The only noise was the lapping of the water upon the beach and the occasional cracking of seashells under our feet. I picked up a stick and helped a jellyfish back into the water. Matthew threw a rock at a tin can floating on the bay. A flock of seagulls followed us searching for food. I jumped on some dry kelp. It snapped and popped. I stepped from one rock to the other trying not to touch the sand. Matthew floated a dry clam shell on the water. We counted to six before it sunk.

"I'm going up on the mainland," said Matthew suddenly. "Toronto."

I stared at the clam shell rocking back and forth underneath the water. "Toronto? When?"

"Tomorrow."

I didn't expect Matthew would want to leave so soon. I was certain he would spend the rest of the summer at home, at least.

"Yes. Lot's of work up there," he said. "Good chance to move ahead too. Especially with a high school diploma."

A lump the size of an egg formed in my throat. I swallowed and swallowed but it wouldn't go away. With my back to Matthew, I looked across the bay at nothing in particular. I quickly wiped a tear away. "How will you get there?"

"By train," he said. "Got to take the ferry to Nova Scotia first."

"Will you write?"

"Yes."

"Promise?"

"I promise," said Matthew, sitting down on a flat rock.

"Does Becky know?"

Matthew squinted into the sunlight. "No, I haven't told her yet," he said.

Matthew and Becky still seemed to be no more than close friends. To me, they were the perfect couple, relaxed around each other, laughing and joking. I suspected Becky was waiting for Matthew to make the first move. Matthew, on the other hand, was waiting for Becky.

"Becky and Jason will miss you."

"I'll miss them too."

"That's all? You'll miss them?"

Matthew gave me the indulgent smile he always used when he thought I was being dramatic.

"Listen." I said. "Becky's in love with you."

That caught him off guard. He took the longest time brushing the sand off his pants. Then he looked at me strangely. "Really?"

"Sometimes, Matthew Dearing, you are so naive."

"And you so wise for your years, I suppose?"

I threw my arms around him. "I'm going to miss you, Matthew," I said and planted a big kiss on his cheek. "You are better then any brother a girl could ever have." This time I didn't even try to hide my tears.

Matthew hugged me back. He said nothing. He didn't need to.

"I'll keep an eye on Becky and Jason for you," I said, sniffing.

"Thanks, Patience," he said, tickling my chin. "Now dry up those tears for Uncle Matthew."

We headed back home in silence. I was thinking about all of the good times we had on this beach when we were very little, in those innocent times when leaving had never entered our minds.

Next morning as soon as the sun was up, the Dearing household was awake. Nan, sobbing, made breakfast while neighbours stopped by to wish Matthew well. Pap smoked, pacing back and forth. I followed Matthew from room to room as he packed his last items.

Just as he was leaving Becky rushed up to the car and kissed Matthew lightly on the lips. "Take care of yourself," she said. "And write when you're settled."

"I will," he said, smiling and blushing.

I winked at Matthew. He winked back, then Mr. Jackson's car drove off with Matthew inside.

I wiggled my way in between Nan and Pap, watching a cloud of dust long after the car was out of sight. "He'll be back sooner then you think," I said. "Give him till Christmas at the most."

Pap looked at Nan and said, "Dry up dose tears, me dear, I thinks Patience is onto something."

Matthew's leaving was like someone had died in our family. I missed him terribly. We all did. Nothing seemed to be the same. His letters told us he was living in a boarding house, with some men who worked at the same teabag factory. Things were going well. "I am saving all of my money, spending only enough to survive," he wrote.

Soon it was Christmas and Matthew was still in Toronto. Nan and Pap and I went through the motions but our hearts were not in it. At Holy Communion on Christmas Day, I prayed Matthew would come home soon. Boxing Day came and went. Not a single word from him since early December. The mailman said the winter storms on the mainland were mighty bad. It was likely Matthew's letters were hung up along the way.

On New Year's night, Nan put on a bit of a time to welcome in the new year. Mr. Edwards played the accordion, David the spoons and Mrs. Edwards sang. The rest of us danced to the music. Eventually Jason fell asleep on the couch.

Knock! Knock! Knock!

"I wonder who dat could be," said Nan, eyes dancing. "Mummers?"

Nan was about to open the door, when it swung open.

"Merry Christmas, everybody," said a familiar voice, with a hint of Torontonian accent.

"Matthew!" Nan yelled, arms reaching towards him.

Matthew dropped his suitcases on the kitchen floor. "I made it," he said.

Pap jumped up and greeted Matthew, handing him a drink. "So good to see you, me son."

I raced over and kissed Matthew on the cheek. "You had me worried."

"Didn't think you had time to think about anyone but James Jackson these days," said Matthew, hugging me. I'd foolishly mentioned that I thought James was very cute in one of my letters. "You've grown so much, Patience."

"She looks more like her poor mother every day," Nan said.

In all of the excitement, Matthew didn't see Becky right away.

"It's good to see you," she said.

The way Matthew's eyes lit up, I could tell that's who he really came home to see. Without any hesitation he scooped Becky up and spun her around the kitchen.

"Let's have a toast!" said Pap. He brought out his special bottle of spirits and handed a shot glass to everyone.

"Just a little drop for Patience, Tom," said Nan.

"A little drink on special occasions won't hurt no one," said Pap. "Down with it, Patience, tis a special night after all." With Matthew home we really had cause to celebrate.

Matthew told us he had intended to be home for Christmas Eve, but got caught up in the snowstorm. He talked about Toronto, his job and the different things he had done and seen.

I watched Becky sizing up Matthew. Clearly, he had lost all traces of his boyish looks in the last six months. He sported a black moustache now and it was easy to see that his baby face of yesterday could easily grow a full beard, if given half a chance. His chest seemed broader than it used to be. Black hair stuck out through his v-neck shirt. I wondered if Becky liked the transformation. My guess was, she did.

With all of the celebration, we didn't realize that it was morning until Jason woke up. "Mom, why did we stay here all night?" he said, rubbing the sleep from his eyes.

"Matthew came home last night," said Becky.

"Mew came home? Mew is here?" He raced towards Matthew. "Santa Claus finally brought me the present I asked for. But he was some late!"

CHAPTER 25

The Telegram

THE HOLIDAYS WERE OVER. Matthew was going back to Toronto tomorrow. Nan was darning one last pair of socks while Matthew packed. "I wish you didn't have to go back, me son," she said.

"Warehouse Supervisor is one of the best jobs in the factory," said Matthew, closing his suitcase. "And the people I work with treats me well."

"Seems to me you'd rather be in Newfoundland," I said.

"It's hard to get used to their way of life," Matthew said. "Everything is planned and done by invitation. Everyone is too busy getting by."

"What?" said Nan. "Can't drop by a friend's place for a good laugh and a bite to eat, whenever you please. Name of God, what kind of a place is it den when you can't stop in fer a cut of tea, unannounced?"

"Oh, it takes a bit of getting use to," said Matthew. "Once in a while, on a Friday night, I go out to the club with a few of the boys from work."

"That's why your social life was nothing to write home about," I said. "Silly me, thinking you were picking up all of these girls in the clubs and at the factory. Not like you and Becky were going steady or anything."

Matthew pushed me off the bed, where I'd been sitting next to him, watching him pack. "I was wondering when you'd get back at me for mentioning James Jackson the other night," he said.

"Da two of you will never grow up," said Nan, shaking her head.

"Are you telling me that you and Becky are a real couple now?"

"Looks that way, Patience," said Matthew. He grabbed my hand and pulled me to my feet. "One of these days I'll be coming back home to marry her."

"Oh son," said Nan. "Dat's good news, indeed."

Matthew looked out over the frozen winterland. "Leaving this time is far more difficult," he said. "The thought of living in Toronto, without Becky and Jason, leaves me cold to the bone."

That night though, old man winter saw fit to blow up a gale force wind, dumping six feet of fresh snow on an already ten-foot-high base. Temperatures dropped to fifty below. Pap said it was cold enough for spit to freeze before it hit the ground.

"Looks like da weather we had da winter Patience was born," Nan said, shivering. "I pray dere is no poor woman having a baby tonight."

"Don't look like Matthew will make it back from Becky's," I said.

Five days later, things were back to normal and Matthew left for Toronto.

From inside Nan and I admired the snow-covered frozen land, the deep blue sky and the bright sunlight. Trees and fences were completely buried. A shovelled path, leading to the door of the woodhouse, was the

The Telegram

only indication that a building existed fifty feet away. Snow, piled high on both sides of the main road, verified the snow-plow had been through earlier. Pap, hidden by the snowbanks, was tossing snow over his head as he shovelled a path from the house to the main road. Crystal icicles hung from the edge of the roof, and through the living room window I watched them cry little droplets as the sun slowly melted them away.

I was thinking of Matthew on his way to Toronto. I wondered if I, too, would be living in a big city after I graduated this coming June.

"Who's dat man?" said Nan, pointing towards the main road.

The overweight stranger, dressed like a man of importance, had one leg free while the other was stuck in the snow up to his hip. Snow clung to the brown and orange wool scarf wrapped around his neck, telling us he had fallen a lot. With both hands, he pulled the brim of his flattened fedora down over his fat, red face.

"Reminds me of a clown." I was trying to cheer Nan up.

"Patience, you's awful," said Nan, laughing despite herself. "You shouldn't be poking fun at dat poor man."

Suddenly Nan stopped laughing.

"What's wrong?"

"Suppose something happened to Matthew!"

We both grabbed our coats and boots, and hurried outside.

"Tom!"

Pap looked up startled. "My Lord, Rose, what's da matter?"

"Who was dat man and what did he want? Did something happen to Matthew?"

Pap threw his shovel aside. "Rose Dearing, you's something else. Come here, me darling. Come here."

Nan calmed down, but she was still upset. "I worry about every little thing," she said. Then she picked up a handful of snow, threw it at Pap, and tried to run.

Pap caught her. They both fell together in the soft white blanket provided by Mother Nature. They rolled around and giggled like children.

"Well, who was he and what did he want?" said Nan, when they both lay exhausted.

"I'll tell you if you give me a great big kiss," said Pap.

"Tom, stop being foolish. Patience's right dere watching," she said, pointing to me.

Pap's mouth covered hers and they kissed. But not for long.

Not wanting the fun to stop, I picked up two huge handfuls of snow and dropped it on their heads. "Patience Dearing," said Pap, bolting upright and tripping me on top of him and Nan. I had never seen his eyes twinkle as much as they did then.

"Let's git her," giggled Nan, throwing a handful of snow towards me.

The stranger turned out to be a Mr. Duffy from the provincial government in St. John's. He happened to be in Dearing Bay on another matter, and had hoped to see Matthew in response to a job application. The job was Matthew's, if he wanted it, but he had to let Mr. Duffy know in the next few weeks.

The Telegram

"Read Matthew's telegram one more time, Nan, please," I said.

It was long past our usual bedtime and we were still sitting around the kitchen table. Nan reached into her apron pocket for the yellow telegram, delivered just before sunset by the postmistress. "Spoke with Mr. Duffy. Accepted offer for April 1st. Arrive home March 21st. Love. Matthew."

CHAPTER 26

The Wedding

DAVID AND I WERE SITTING on the beach, listening to Nan and Mrs. Edwards chatting about Matthew and Becky's upcoming wedding, and my graduation, and how sad Nan was that her babies were all grown up. Then Mrs. Edwards told Nan about Hilda Mae wanting David to quit school and go to Toronto with her.

This was news to me.

"Yeah," said David, letting sand run through his fingers. "Hilda Mae says she's going with or without me. If I don't make up my mind by tonight, she'll take someone else to the graduation dance."

"What are you going to do?"

"Don't know yet. Got any suggestions?"

"School is important. You might regret quitting later on."

"I know," said David.

Neither of us spoke for quite awhile. I couldn't imagine what it would be like without David. First Matthew. Now David!

"Who are you going to the dance with, Patience? James or Fred?"

"Maybe neither," I said.

David thought I was kidding.

"I like them both equally," I said. "Fred's funny and James is a gentleman. They both want me to go steady but I don't have that special feeling for them, that people talk about."

"What do you mean?"

"My heart doesn't race and I don't see shooting stars when they kiss me. To tell you the truth, I can't wait for their kisses to end."

I'd always told David what I was thinking but, this time, I caught him off guard. He glanced around to see if his grandmother and Nan were listening. I'd probably embarrassed him but there was something I needed to know. "You've been going out with Hilda Mae for a long time, what should it feel like?"

David screwed up his nose. "Feel like?"

"You know – kissing," I said. "When Fred kissed me I felt like laughing. With James, all I noticed was his teeth biting into my lip. Is that as good as it gets?"

David doodled in the sand. "At first it was really nice. Now it's different. I don't know. Hilda Mae has changed." David whirled a rock out to sea as hard as he could. "It's confusing."

I put my arm around David's shoulder. "It was a whole lot more fun when you and I were out in the bay with that old black dory," I said, pointing to the wreck on the beach. "When we were ten or eleven."

"I wouldn't mind those days back again," said David. "Remember the time you banged a pound of nails in your Nan's doorstep and blamed it on Matthew?"

"Don't say it too loud," I said, laughing. "Nan still thinks it was Matthew right to this day."

The Wedding

We watched our ducks waddle down the beach and into the water.

"So," said David. "What am I going to tell Hilda Mae?"

I feared David would be pressured into something he'd regret.

"Tell her you're going to finish high school," I said. "And tell her you're going to the dance with me."

"Are you serious?"

"Absolutely."

The first few weeks of June sped by. Nan, Becky and I worked nearly around the clock getting everything ready for the wedding. We decorated the village church from top to bottom. "The same church Tom and I got married in," said Nan. "Close to forty years ago."

Mrs. Edwards brought a special arrangement of daffodils. She picked them from her garden. She told Nan that David had dropped Hilda Mae like a hot spud.

Becky was insisting on a quiet, simple wedding with only the immediate family in attendance. Nan warned her it was likely the whole village would show up, including Mrs. Adams, God forbid.

Nan was right. On the wedding day the church was packed to the doors. Matthew, dressed in a blue suit and white tie, stood at the alter next to David, his best man. Mrs. Gibbs pumped out *Here Comes the Bride* at the organ. Becky wearing the same teal-blue dress she wore to Matthew's graduation, came down the aisle on her father's arm.

"Mom, you look some pretty," shouted Jason.

Reverend Gibbs began the wedding ceremony. "Do you take this man to be your lawful wedded husband?"

"She looks in da family way to me, got that special glow," said Mrs. Adams, in a stage whisper.

David glanced at me, standing next to Becky.

"I do," said Becky, voice quivering. It was obvious she had heard Mrs. Adams, as had most of the congregation.

Nan sobbed louder and harder.

Matthew's face flushed as red as a cherry, but in a steady voice he promised to love, honour and cherish.

Was there any truth in Mrs. Adams' words?

Outside the church, Matthew and Becky were showered with rice for good luck and warm wishes. I was certain in my heart that Becky and Matthew's life would be one terrific love story, just like Nan and Pap's.

In the early morning, while guests were still celebrating just outside my room, I crawled into bed. I was exhausted, but couldn't sleep. Strangely, I kept thinking about the time I told David I didn't want to ride my bike through the potholes with him. Did he feel then the way I did now? Alone and deserted?

Nan had cried at the church today. I understood her heartbreak in the midst of one of the happiest moments of her life. Becky and Jason were Matthew's family now. They would become the greater part of his life. Nan, Pap and I would have to settle for less. Tears spilled down my cheeks. Like Nan, I was happy and heartbroken at the same time.

My world would never be the same.

CHAPTER 27

Always in Your Heart

"Don't tell me Matthew took time out of his honeymoon to write you," said Pap, handing me an envelope.

I knew very well it wasn't from Matthew. I'd been looking forward to this letter for close to a month. My heart pounded. What if it wasn't the news I'd longed for?

"Well, open it up," said Nan. "Tell me what Matthew and Becky is up too."

I ripped open the envelope and read the letter to myself. "Yes! Yes! Yes!"

"You'll wet yur bloomers if you keeps jumping up and down, like that." said Nan. "Lord 'ave mercy, Tom, the girl's gone giddy on us."

"I've been accepted for university," I cried, dancing around my grandparents with the letter in my hand. "St. John's in September."

"Well," said Nan, sitting down. "Dat's jest like you, Patience. Not telling me what you was up too." Her face suddenly became sober. "I's happy fer you, Patience, but it's hard to take. First Matthew. Now you." She wiped her eyes with the corner of her apron. "I wish da two of you was just babies, crawling around me feet."

"I can stay with Matthew and Becky," I said. "Until I get settled."

"I think tis a good thing you's going to get more learning," said Pap. "I dare say you'll be the best teacher dat ever stepped foot in Dearing Bay, one of dese days."

Then in walked David, dressed in a fine suit.

I'd been so excited about my news that I'd completely forgotten about the time. "Give me a minute and I'll be ready." I raced into my bedroom. Clothes flew everywhere. I grabbed my new floor-length dress and hauled it over my head. I threw on my never-worn shiny shoes, and quickly brushed my hair. Thank goodness, I had washed it earlier in the day. I smudged a little rouge on my cheeks, dabbed mascara on my eyelashes and slicked my lips with a light pink lipstick. I took one quick check in the mirror, grabbed my bag and ran out to David.

At the school, I was so pleased to see Ruth Gower and Michael Sutherland together. Ruth glowed from head to toe. Michael held her hand most of the time. Fred and James each had dates, girls from David's class. Hilda Mae, without a date, was by herself on the other side of the gym.

"Beautiful Patience Dearing," said Fred, standing up to greet us. He slapped David on the back. "You lucky dog."

I looked across at Hilda Mae. One of our classmates, obviously alone too, had joined her. Tony kept his head down, trying to cover his face during their conversation. He'd been self-conscious of his acne since the day he walked in the school. Hilda Mae kept glancing toward us. She looked miserable.

"David, what'd you say if we'd asked Hilda Mae and Tony to join us?" I couldn't believe what I was saying. I was the last person to feel sorry for Hilda Mae.

"You'd better ask her," said David.

"The more the merrier," said Fred, pulling me to my feet. "You and I will ask them, Patience Dearing."

Hilda Mae's mouth fell open when Fred asked her and Tony to join us. Nothing came out. Miracles do happen, I thought.

"I need one more beautiful girl at my table," said Fred. Then he said it was my idea.

"What about David?" said Hilda Mae, looking at me.

"How about if we let the evening unfold?" I said. "There's no reason why we can't all be friends."

It was awkward at first, but by the time the opening ceremonies were over, we were all talking about our high school years, the good times and the bad times. We laughed, and occasionally choked back our tears. David and Hilda Mae were talking to each other, and I noticed Tony didn't keep his hands over his face so much.

After dinner when the music began James and Fred were immediately on the floor with their dates. There was an uncomfortable pause while Hilda Mae looked at David, then at me.

"Let's dance," said Tony.

Hilda Mae smiled, and followed him out on the crowded dance floor.

We danced to all the songs, slow and fast. We switched partners back and forth – sometimes boys with boys and girls with girls. All too soon, it was the final song of the evening.

"Patience, will you have the last dance with me?" said David.

"Thought you'd never ask," I said.

Hilda Mae and Tony were wrapped around each other, necking as they danced. So were Ruth and Michael.

"I had a good time tonight," said David. "I'm really glad you asked me."

"What are friends for?" I said.

After, we gathered at our table for our final goodbyes.

"So what's everyone doing this summer?" I said. "Or for the rest of their lives?" I added cheerfully. I hoped no one could tell how I really felt. I was as sad as the night Matthew got married.

"I'm off to Dalhousie University," said Michael. "Ruth is going to join me as soon as she finishes secretary college." Ruth hugged me, promising to keep in touch.

James said he was going to engineering school in Halifax. Hilda Mae had dropped any thought of Toronto and was now thinking of working her way across Europe with Tony.

"I'm going on the high seas," said Fred, raising both arms over his head. "Yeah. Fishing with me uncle."

"Why am I not surprised?" I said.

"Guess I'm back at Spectrum High for one final year," said David, smiling at me.

Fred tugged my hair. "What about you Patience Dearing?"

"St. John's. Off to university to be a teacher." David gasped. I hadn't told him about my letter. "Got word today," I said.

"Patience Dearing," said Fred. "You'll make one heck of a teacher."

On the bus ride home, I remembered the first day I stepped foot inside the yellow container. All of us on top of each other. How young we were two short years ago. David and I got out in front of my house.

"I feel like kissing you," he said. "But I care too much for our friendship to risk losing it."

David couldn't be serious! But for a split second, I wondered what it would be like. Like Fred or James or something entirely different?

"Friendship is everything, David," I said. "Thanks for a wonderful night."

"Patience...."

"Yes."

"Nothing. I'll see you tomorrow."

David stood at the gate, watching until I was at my door. "Tomorrow," I said.

Before I turned in, I slipped into Nan and Pap's bedroom, just like I did when I was a little girl. "Are you awake?" I said.

They moved over to make room for me in between them. "Thanks for making me the beautiful dress, Nan. I felt lovely in it tonight."

"You is welcome, me love."

"We had such a good time tonight. All of us dancing together," I said. "I'm going to miss them."

"I knows dat you will, Patience," said Pap.

"It was sad saying goodbye," I said, snuggling down between them. "I may never see some of my friends ever again."

"Dey will always be in yur heart, me dear," Pap said.

"Just like my poor mother is always in your heart, Pap?"

"Yes, dat's da way tis – always dere whenever you want dem to be."

"Your Pap is right, Patience," said Nan. "Jest think of the good memories when yur heart is heavy in yur body, my child."

I woke up to sunshine streaming in the window. Nan and Pap were already up. I lay still and listened to the world around me. Robins, blue jays and sparrows were singing melodies in the warm outdoors. Waves lapped upon the shoreline, interrupted for a short time by the putt-putt sound of a fisherman's boat making its way down the bay. The sound of sheep baaing over the hill was cut off by a car roaring up the gravel road. Little children, playing down by the water's edge, squealed in delight. Pap dropped the lid on the wood stove, and his and Nan's soft voices floated into the bedroom while they talked over their morning tea.

It dawned on me that life was like a story book. Innocent chapters of our lives had ended and exciting chapters were about to begin. Today was the beginning of a brand new section. It was up to me to make my role as interesting and as wonderful as the chapters of my childhood.

Always in Your Heart

I jumped out of bed and rushed to the open window. I shouted out across all that was dear and familiar to me. "Hello world – here I come!"

My grandparents, sitting side by side at the breakfast table, smiled when I entered the kitchen.

"She's jest like her father," said Nan.

"More like her mother, I'd say," said Pap.

Throwing my arms around their necks, I planted big kisses on both their cheeks. "Me thinks I's got the best of me Nan and Pap."